THEY WENT FOR
THEIR GUNS...

Jessie saw a battered Winchester leaning up against the wall, and she leapt for it.

"Here!" she yelled, tossing it to Ki as she yanked a sixshooter from the station tender's skinny hips.

Together they charged back out the doorway with bullets whipping all around them. They dove in behind the water trough. Jessie got off the first wild shot as the rope tightened around the Mexican's neck. The rider spurred his horse off at a hard run, dragging the body of the Mexican behind him.

Her first bullet missed, but her second made the roper stand up in his stirrups. Ki's first rifle shot knocked him out of the saddle. His horse bolted and ran, dragging the Mexican across the meadow.

Ki dropped the Winchester and took off running.

Jessie grabbed the rifle and fired at the remaining gunmen. One turned his horse and raced for the hills, but the other charged the onrushing samurai with his sixgun blazing. . . .

WESLEY ELLIS

LONE STAR

AND THE ARIZONA GUNMEN

JOVE BOOKS, NEW YORK

LONE STAR AND THE ARIZONA GUNMEN

A Jove Book/published by arrangement with
the author

PRINTING HISTORY
Jove edition/March 1990

ISBN: 0-515-10271-7

Jove Books are published by The Berkley Publishing Group,
200 Madison Avenue, New York, New York 10016.
The name "JOVE" and the "J" logo
are trademarks belonging to Jove Publications, Inc.

PRINTED IN THE UNITED STATES OF AMERICA

10 9 8 7 6 5 4 3 2 1

Chapter 1

The wind was blowing across the Mogollon Rim country of eastern Arizona, and it was hot wind, the kind that dried the sweat on your forehead before it could river down and sting your eyes.

Jessica Starbuck studied the hard land through the window of the rocking Concord stage with interest. She had heard that there were big cattle and sheep ranches in this part of the country and that there was also the threat of a range war between them.

Jessie frowned. Given the bleak but starkly beautiful high mesas and the dry, broken mountains, she figured that it would take an awful lot of land to keep a cow fat. Maybe a hundred acres. It would be much better for sheep, but even with woollies, it looked to Jessie that this was a country where profits would be mighty thin even in the best of years.

Unfortunately, ranchers were not having the best of years. Beef prices were down and and so were those for lamb and mutton. But the wool market was stronger than it ever had been, and that had set Jessie to thinking that she might just diversify her Starbuck Enterprises into running forty or fifty thousand head of sheep.

Jessie smiled at the thought of how the foreman of her immense Texas Circle Star cattle ranch would be appalled to learn of her plans to incorporate sheep into the Starbuck Enterprises. Ed Wright felt the same way about sheep as most cattlemen—he hated the stinking, bleating beggars.

"What are you smiling about?" the handsome, dark-eyed man across from her asked.

Ki was her friend and protector. A few years older than Jessie, he was dressed in a loose-fitting black costume and wore a braided leather headband. Ki was half-white, the son of a seafaring American, and half-Japanese, the son of a beautiful Nipponese princess who had paid with her life for falling in love with someone judged unworthy by her venerable family.

"Was I smiling?"

"Yes," Ki said. "You were looking out the window at this hard country and then, quite suddenly, you smiled."

"I was thinking of buying sheep and some good grazing land. Perhaps even some in these parts."

"What is so amusing about that?" asked Ki. Jessie owned ranches all over the world.

"Well, then I thought about the reaction of Ed Wright and our Lone Star cowboys," Jessie added. "They would be outraged and likely stage a cowboy rebellion."

Ki allowed himself a smile. He was samurai and, therefore, more reserved than most white people. But he did have a dry and very refined sense of humor, and he could see it in the situation that Jessie had just described.

"A real Texas cowboy would rather shovel manure all day than touch a woolly," he conceded.

"They seem to have such a monumental disgust for them," Jessie said.

2

"Sheep are very stupid."

Jessie nodded. "That's true, but cattle aren't the smartest animals God put in this world, either."

"And sheep are greasy and they stink," Ki said.

Jessie cocked one eyebrow upward. She had green eyes, reddish-blond hair, and the figure of a Greek love goddess. When she laughed, her voice was music, and when she was upset, her eyes seemed to throw off glittering sparks of anger. "You sound like the cowboys," she said.

"I'm not a cowboy, you know that."

"But you sound like them," Jessie repeated. "Ki, first, last, and always, I am a businesswomen. If sheep can make me more money than cattle right now, then I'll run sheep. I don't have to like the sound, the sight, the touch, or the feel of their greasy wool. The only thing that matters is that they are profitable."

"You own dozens of profitable companies around the world. Last year we bought another rubber plantation in South America, a silver mine in Alaska, and a diamond mine in South Africa. We also bought two railroads, one in Spain and . . ."

Jessie held up her hand. "I know what I bought. What is your point?"

"My point," Ki said, "is that you are worth more money than some entire countries. So why bother with sheep if you admit they are so disagreeable?"

"Because," Jessie answered, "everything can turn around. If you allow yourself to lose money in one operation, pretty soon you might do the same in another. I pay my employees the highest wages, and I expect performance. I give millions of dollars to charity, and I want to continue to do so. I cannot do that if I am losing money."

"So," Ki said, "you are trying to tell me that one unprofitable enterprise could be like the hole in the dike. At

3

first the water escapes in only a dribble, then it becomes a gushing torrent, and finally the entire dam collapses and is washed away."

"Yes!" Jessie said. "That is a good analogy. One I'll have to remember to use the next time I am forced to come down hard on one of my managers for showing me an unprofitable year."

Ki could not hide a smile. "Forgive them if they, like me, find the whole idea of the Starbuck empire crumbling away like some earthen dam amusing. Before your father's death, he used that analogy and it didn't go over any better then than it would now."

Jessie was surprised. "Really?"

"Yes," Ki said. "He came up with it when one of his shipping lines showed an annual loss."

"And?"

Ki shrugged. "You knew him better than I did."

"Yes, but I wasn't there when he used the analogy. What happened?"

"He was speaking before the entire board of directors and the company officials. They all started laughing at once."

"At my father?" Jessie could not believe that. Alex Starbuck was not a man that anyone had ever laughed at, only with.

"Yes," Ki said. "You see, the company had been profitable for three years running, and in the year that your father used that analogy, they had only lost two hundred dollars."

"Two hundred dollars!"

"Yes," Ki said. "And when your father made the analogy and they all laughed, he began to laugh with them. The next year, however, that shipping line made him almost a quarter of a million dollars in profit after taxes."

4

"That's my father," Jessie said with pride as her mind drifted back over the years.

Alex Starbuck had been a self-made man. He'd gotten his start in a tiny importing and exporting business in San Francisco. As that business expanded, Alex had bought a battered sailing ship to carry merchandise from Japan and China to the Barbary Coast. Soon he'd added a second ship, and within a few years he had a fleet. Everything that Jessie's father touched had turned to gold. He'd had a sixth sense about opportunity, and he'd been an innovator when he'd bought the first iron-hulled steamer on the Pacific Coast. Because iron had been extravagantly expensive and the steamer had proved far superior to the wooden hulls used by his jealous competitors, Alex had bought his own mill, as well as mines to supply it with iron ore.

Not content with owning one of the largest steamlines in the world, Alex had also embraced the railroads. His mills, which had turned out iron hulls for his expanding fleet, also began to make steel rails, and when the banks could not supply his capital needs, he started his own banks and brokerage houses.

Alex Starbuck had lost count of his net worth by the time he was forty. But there were others who saw him with the eyes of a predator. They'd needed Alex to form a cartel of businessmen whose twisted intent was to seize control of the economic muscle of the world. To set up their own financial systems and political dynasties. And Alex, the key to this diabolical plan of world domination, had scorned the cartel and set about to expose it.

For this, Alex had been ruthlessly murdered—but not before he had ruined the cartel and destroyed its grand and demented design to achieve world domination.

"Jessie?"

5

She turned from the window and looked at the samurai. "Yes?"

"You're thinking about him, aren't you?"

"How did you know?"

Ki leaned forward and touched her arm. "You're so much like your father that it is as easy for me to read your mind as it was his."

"If that's so," Jessie said, "then what would he think about the Circle Star Ranch owning forty or fifty thousand head of sheep?"

"If they were money-makers," Ki said, "he'd have done it in a moment. Just as you will."

Jessie sighed. "Thanks for your honesty," she said. "There are many people who try to guess what I want to hear and then say it, but, fortunately, you aren't one of them. I can always count on you for a truthful and well-reasoned response. You're not only my friend, companion, and protector, you're my sounding board."

Jessie touched his cheek. He'd saved her life on more than one occasion, and he was the only person in the world she'd trust with her life. "Ki, I'd be lost without you by my side."

Ki was not visibly moved the way some men would have been. The samurai had too much control over his emotions to allow himself a display of emotion, but Jessie knew that he was touched by her words.

"Butte Station coming up!" the stagecoach driver yelled out into the high mountain air. "Be staying here for the noonday meal, Miss Starbuck!"

"Good," Jessie said. "I'm famished."

Ki was, too. They had not eaten since the night before, and it had been a long, long night in the coach.

Jessie leaned her head out of the window and gazed up ahead toward Butte Station. She observed two pole corrals, several broken-down wagons, a log cabin resting in a fine meadow, and three saddle horses tied up at a hitching rail. A large black and white border collie was resting in the shade of a pine tree beside a man wearing a sombrero with its brim tipped down over his face.

"Doesn't look like much," she said to the samurai. "I just hope that whoever is cooking has something besides chili and beef."

"It is getting a little monotonous," Ki said. "That's about all we've had since leaving San Diego."

"This is sheep country," Jessie said. "Perhaps they'll have mutton or lamb chops."

Ki also peered out the window. "Don't count on it," he said, pulling his head back inside. "Those horses that are tied up at the hitching rail belong to cowboys. It's not likely that they'll be cooking anything but beef at this station."

Jessie figured the samurai was probably right. But maybe they'd have something besides beef, which tended to get a little monotonous, even to a cattle rancher.

When the stage rolled to a stop, Ki hopped out and offered Jessie his hand and then helped her down, though she would have preferred to get down on her own.

Jessie was wearing a light cotton dress because of the heat, and she scorned the use of a parasol or bonnet. Her shoes were not the fashionable high-heeled kind with laces running up over the ankles, but were instead flat-heeled and made for walking. Beautiful, yes; fancy or delicate, she was not.

Jessie most enjoyed wearing blue denims, a loose but comfortable man's shirt, and a pair of cowboy boots. She had practically been raised on horseback, and she was an expert, having been taught from childhood by the Circle Star vaqueros how to handle horses and a rope. She was also a dead-shot with a sixgun, thanks to her father's insistence that she become a marksman with both a pistol and a rifle.

"It sure isn't much, is it?" she said, stretching the stiffness out of her long, shapely legs and eyeing the men and the log cabin where they were apparently supposed to be eating.

Ki immediately noted the three cowboys who were leering at Jessie. In a rough country like this, you found rough men without manners. Jessie was a woman and you could not blame men for staring at her, but if they became coarse or aggressive, then it was time to draw the line. And with these three, Ki already had the premonition that the line would be crossed.

"Well, hello!" the biggest of the cowboys said, a wide and lascivious grin creasing his lips as he stepped up and blocked Jessie's forward progress. "Now, damn me if you ain't a picture for sore eyes! My, my, but you are a looker, woman! I sure would like to make your acquaintance."

Jessie met his eyes. "Get out of my way," she said quietly.

The man's eyebrows raised and his grin slipped a notch. "Now, missy! That sure ain't being mannerly. No, sir, not at all!"

Ki moved in closer to Jessie. His face was a hard mask, but his voice was soft, almost casual. "The lady asked you to step aside," he said. "I think you'd better do it right now."

The tall cowboy had ignored the samurai up to that moment, but now he turned and looked down at Ki with leering contempt. "Listen, you Chinaman sonofa—"

He never finished what he'd started to say. As fast as an eyeblink, Ki's right hand blurred and the iron-hard muscles in the edge of his tensed hand chopped down and hit the tall man at the base of the neck. The motion was a blur and very much like the swing of an axe.

The effect was also the same. The tall man's eyes rolled up into his forehead and his legs buckled like wet paper as he collapsed with a groan.

For an instant the other two hard cases could only stare in disbelief, then they cursed and attacked.

Jessie stepped back, her hand slipping inside the pocket of her dress and finding a two-shot derringer. She was certain that she would not have to use it, but just the feel of the gun in her fist was reassuring.

The two men sprang at the samurai, who had bounced back after the delivery of his devastating blow to stand with his legs slightly bent, his hands upraised and slightly extended from his body in the *te* or hand fighting position that he had been taught as an orphan in Japan.

Ki waited until the first man sprang at him, and then his foot lashed upward in a sweep lotus that caught the attacker in the throat and dropped him choking to the ground.

The third man was wiser, and he had a fraction of a second more time. His fist exploded against the side of Ki's head, and the samurai crashed over backward in the dirt as the man jumped at him with every intention of stomping him to death with his heavy boots. Ki rolled and came up with his ears ringing. "Nice punch," he said grudgingly. "Why don't you try that again now that I can give you my undivided attention?"

The man was short, but barrel-chested and heavily muscled. He had a broken nose and an ugly knife scar across one cheek, and now he reached for his gun.

"Don't!" Jessie said, pulling the derringer out of her dress and cocking it loudly.

The man glanced aside at her, then swore and said, "I

9

reckon I can handle this fancy-fisted Chinaman with my bare hands."

Ki lifted his weight on the balls of his feet, and when the man came wading in with his fists, Ki ducked and thundered two powerful uppercuts to the body. It was like punching a draft horse, and Ki took a sledgehammer-like punch to the side of the head that sent him reeling.

The man roared a challenge and then lashed out with a kick of his own that was meant to crush the samurai's testicles like grapes. Ki caught the boot at the apex of its arc, and he twisted it hard, dropping his opponent heavily to the dirt and knocking the air out of his lungs.

"Get up," Ki said.

The man looked up at the samurai with disbelief. "You're going to let me up?"

"Yeah."

"Why?"

"Because I have no fear of you," Ki said. "And when I beat you, I want you to know that it wasn't luck or a fluke."

The man blinked and sleeved his mouth. "I'll say this, you are a cocky bastard. But you just made the biggest mistake of your yellow life."

Ki waited until the man was erect, and then he went after him. A jarring snap-kick to the chin sent the man crashing up against the log cabin, and then Ki grabbed him by the shirtfront, jerked him completely off the ground. He drove the man's thick head into the hitching post, then caught him and dumped him into the water trough.

The samurai stepped back and looked at the wide-eyed station tender. "Is dinner ready?"

"Why . . . why, yeah. Sure is!"

Ki nodded. "We've had nothing but chili and beef since

we left San Diego four days ago. I hope you've got something different."

The station tender swallowed noisily and wrung his hands in a gesture of despair. No words were necessary. The menu was chili and beef.

Chapter 2

The chili was fire-hot and the table, plates, and utensils so dirty that Ki took them outside and washed them in the horse's watering trough. The three hard cases he'd whipped were still hanging around, and the samurai eyed them closely because he half-expected them to draw their guns and open fire. But they didn't, and so Ki went back inside the log cabin to eat.

The station tender was a thin, hook-nosed man in his forties who had watery eyes and bad teeth. He wore a dirty apron and had a cold or an allergy because he kept sniffling and sleeving his running nose. His hostler was of the same ilk, only twenty years younger and as hungry as a lobo wolf. The older man's name was Milo and the younger man was called Arnie.

"Yes, sir!" Milo said, pointing a spoon at Ki. "I never thought I'd ever seen a Chinaman who would or could fight like you did out there, mister. In fact, I never saw anybody that could fight like that. All them fancy kicks and stuff. Where the hell did you learn 'em?"

"In Japan," Ki said, sitting down to his plate of chili and

fried beef with a fist-sized chunk of sourdough bread.

"In Japan? Why, I never even know'd there was such a place as that! Is it like China? I worked with Chinamen on the Central Pacific Railroad back in sixty-seven. Yes, sir! Them little yellow sonsabitches sure could move some dirt when they was told to. They'd outwork the Irish every time and they'd stay sober, too, by gawd!"

Jessie looked over at the driver. "How far to the next station?"

"Forty mile."

"Do you expect the food will be any better than this?"

"Yes, ma'am, I do. There's a woman there and she kin cook a little."

Jessie pushed her plate away and contented herself with the hard sourdough.

"Right sorry you didn't like my chili, your highness," the station tender said in a huff.

"Better shut up," Arnie said. "If you don't, that friend of hers is likely to do to you what he did to them three outside. It was a sight to see."

Ki said nothing.

Arnie added, "I sure wish I could fight like that. Iff'n I could, reckon I'd whip some ass in these mountains and take me the prettiest girl on the whole derned Mogollon Rim."

"Mind your filthy tongue," Milo snapped. "Less'n the Chinaman pulls a knife and cuts it out for offending the woman."

Jessie chewed her sourdough and brushed absently at the flies that circled overhead and kept landing on the food. "I hear that there is trouble between the cattlemen and the sheepmen in these parts. Is that true?"

"Damn right it is!" Milo exclaimed. "There's trouble

13

aplenty, but it won't be lastin' much longer. Ain't that right, Arnie?" he said with a wink.

Jessie frowned. "Why won't it be lasting much longer?"

The two stagecoach employees snickered. The driver looked away in disgust.

Ki was running low on patience. "The lady asked you a question," he said. "I expect that you'd better answer."

The pair stopped their snickering, and it was Arnie who said, "The cattlemen are gonna wipe out the Mex sheepman. It's acomin' and plain for anybody to see. Why, those three men you whipped was here celebrating when you arrived. They'd just shot a greaser and was fixin' to have themselves some fun with him."

Jessie dropped her sourdough bread. "Are you serious?"

"He sure as hell is," Milo said with a triumphant smirk on his face. "You musta seen the greaser leaning up against that tree yonder."

Jessie came to her feet. "You mean he's been shot? I thought he was just taking a siesta!"

"With three cattlemen around?" Milo chortled as if that were a great joke.

Ki reached out and grabbed the station tender by the shirtfront and dragged him over the table. "Are you saying that man was unconscious and they were going to kill him?"

Milo struggled feebly but his feet were completely off the ground and he was helpless. "Why, yes, sir! That's exactly what they were fixin' to do!"

Ki flung the man aside and pivoted for the open door. He was just in time to see one of the battered cowboys he'd whipped rope the unconscious Mexican.

"Hey!" Ki yelled. "Stop that!"

In response, the other two men opened fire, and Ki

jumped sideways out of the doorway as bullets stitched through the opening.

"A rifle!" he yelled, angry because his bow and arrows were on the stage and he could not get at them.

Jessie saw a battered Winchester leaning up against the wall, and she leapt for it. "Here!" she yelled, tossing it to the samurai, then turned and yanked an old cap and ball sixshooter from the station tender's skinny hips.

Together, they charged back out the doorway with bullets whipping all around them. They both dived in behind the water trough, and it was Jessie who got off the first wild shot as the rope tightened around the Mexican's neck and the rider spurred his horse off at a hard run dragging the body of the Mexican as his dog barked furiously.

Jessie's first bullet missed, but her second made the roper stand up in his stirrups and throw both hands skyward. Ki's first rifle shot knocked him out of the saddle, but the man's rope was tied to his horn and his horse bolted and ran, dragging the Mexican across the meadow.

Ki dropped the Winchester rifle, jumped up, and took off running. He knew that the Mexican was probably already dead, but there was just a chance he might still be alive, and now he was being strangled. . . .

Jessie grabbed the fallen Winchester and tried to lay down a withering fire. If she couldn't actually kill the riders, she at least intended to distract them enough to keep them from gunning down the samurai.

She fired as quickly as she could and the effect was to rattle the two remaining gunmen. One turned his horse and raced for the hills, but the other charged the onrushing samurai with his sixgun blazing.

Jessie held her fire and her breath because the two men came into a direct line.

"Your fightin' friend is a goner," the stage driver said.

"That man on horseback is Duke Lilly, and he's one of the best."

Jessie saw Ki's stride break, and for a split second she thought for sure the samurai had been hit, but then realized that he was reaching into his tunic, and Jessie knew exactly why because the samurai carried *shuriken* star blades inside his tunic. Now, as his arm shot forward, the star blade glittered in the bright Arizona sun as it rotated its deadly course toward the onrushing horseman and struck him in the forehead.

"Jeezus!" the stagecoach driver whispered. "What'd he throw!"

"A *shuriken*," Jessie said as the rider grabbed his forehead, then flipped over backward and hit the earth.

Ki was a blur as he raced across the meadow on a trajectory that would intercept the fear-driven horse, which was bucking and dragging the Mexican. He ripped his thin but very sharp *tanto* blade from its sheath and lunged, not for the horse, but for the taut rope. His blade flashed downward and severed the rope, and the horse bolted away to disappear into the forest.

Ki reached the Mexican first, and when he rolled him over onto his back, he saw, to his amazement, that the man was alive. But his face was purple and his eyes were distended with horror as Ki sliced the choking rope from his twisted neck.

When Jessie reached them, Ki had the Mexican cradled in his arms and was running back toward the station. "He's alive but he needs water," Ki said.

Jessie nodded and ran for water. When she returned, Ki had placed the Mexican down beside the tree, and the dog was whining softly and licking his master's bleeding hand. Jessie knelt beside the dog and stroked its long, silky coat.

The dog was obviously suffering, and it knew the Mexican was going to die.

"Señor," Jessie said in perfect Spanish, "can you hear me?"

The man's eyes fluttered open and he nodded his head, and he surprised them by speaking in English. "My name is Juan Santiago. Please, señor, you must take my body to be blessed and buried beside that of my father."

"Where do you live?"

He tried to raise his hand but failed. "They know," he whispered. "Juan Santiago. Please."

"We will do it," Jessie promised.

But the stage tender had been listening, and he spat, "You can't do that and stay on this coach. Be damned if we're going to wait for you to bury that damned greaser on his ranch!"

Ki came to his feet and his fist exploded into the pit of the man's stomach, doubling him up and making him retch and fold to the ground.

"The man is dying," Ki said in a voice as brittle as ice. "Show a little respect."

Jessie used her handkerchief to bath Juan's poor face. "I am sorry about this," she said. "We thought you were taking a siesta when the stagecoach arrived. If we had known . . ."

The Mexican tried to smile. "It does not matter. I was dying anyway and saying my prayers to God. Now, as I look at you, I see the face of an angel."

His words choked her up and Jessie looked away quickly.

"My dog, señora. Will you also see that he gets back to the ranch? He is a very good dog. His name is Ganso."

"You call him 'goose'?"

A faint chuckle came from the man's rope-mutilated

throat. "*Sí*. He is brave like the goose, and he will bite anyone who steals into his yard."

"I understand."

"Give him to Mando when he returns," Juan whispered. "Tell him to . . . to kill them all!" The Mexican's face contorted and a spasm rocked his body. Jessie heard the man's death rattle, and then he died, and the border collie began to whine louder.

"Damn!" Jessie swore. Then, turning to the hostler, she said, "Where is his ranch?"

"About eighty miles to the north, over by Pine Creek."

"We'll need three saddle horses," she said.

"Can't do that, miss. We just don't have them to sell. They belong to the company, and they ain't for sale at any price. If we sold 'em, we'd lose our jobs and there wouldn't be any fresh horses for the next stage coming through."

"We promised to get this man to his own ranch for burial," Jessie said. "I mean to keep that promise. I'll pay whatever you ask."

"They're not for sale!" the station tender hissed, his arms still wrapped around his midsection and his face twisted with hatred and pain. "You heard Arnie."

"I'd sell 'em my old horse," Arnie offered tentatively. "They could rig a travois and lead my horse over to the Santiago Ranch."

He looked at Ki. "But I have to warn you, there's bad blood between whites and Mex in this country. You go dragging a dead Mex in, and they might just open fire and kill the both of you before you even have a chance to explain."

"Thanks for the warning," Ki said. "But that's a chance we're willing to take."

"How much for your horse?"

18

Arnie swallowed. He glanced at Milo, but the older man looked away with disgust. "Fifty dollars?"

Jessie had no idea what the animal looked like, but she had a hunch it would be a real fleabag and probably not worth even ten dollars. Still, if it would pull the travois to Juan's ranch, then it would be worth the money.

"All right," she said. "Ki, will you rig the travois up to the animal? If we move out within the next half hour, we ought to be able to walk eight miles before dark."

The stagecoach driver said, "I can't wait with the stage for you, miss. I'm sorry, but I got a schedule to keep. I wait for you, then the whole derned run is behind and I get fired."

"That's all right," Jessie said. "We'll catch the next stage through here."

"But that won't come fer almost a week. Not in this direction it won't."

Jessie figured that she'd just have to stay another week and that maybe it would give her and Ki a chance to see more of this country and determine if she wanted to buy a chunk of it for sheep ranching. Still, if men were being shot, she was not sure that she wanted to buy and get herself caught right between the two feuding groups.

Another thing that concerned her was that, in Texas at least, she was regarded as a leader among the cattle ranchers and her Circle Star was a model of efficiency and profitability. Respect from other cattlemen for a woman had been hard-won, and if they found out she had begun to run sheep—even if far-off Arizona—well, she'd be making her share of enemies. But then, on the other hand, Alex Starbuck had taught her that a leader had to do what he thought was best. Only followers and losers put what everyone thought of them first on their list of priorities.

"We'll stay a week," she said, "or we'll buy more

19

horses from the Santiago Ranch and ride out on our own."

"They won't sell a horse to a gringo," the station tender snapped. "You'll find that out quick enough—if you ain't riddled the moment you cross their land."

Jessie turned away from the man. His kind made her sick. They were full of blind hatred and poison for anyone or anything that differed from themselves.

Jessie stroked the dog's head. She was eager to get the hell out of here.

In twenty minutes Arnie's horse was ready and so was the rough travois that Ki had fashioned from aspen poles and a piece of heavy canvas. They picked up the body of Juan Santiago and placed it on the travois, then tied it down.

Jessie dragged out fifty dollars and extended it to Arnie, who surprised her by shaking his head. "Don't seem right to charge that much for my horse," he said. "As you can see, he's not much."

It was true. The horse was swaybacked, underfed, and had a big jug-head and crooked front legs. All together, it was one of the poorest specimens of a horse that Jessie had ever seen, and she would not have allowed it on her ranch, much less ridden the beast.

"Take the fifty," she said, shoving it out at him. "You're right. The horse isn't worth ten dollars under normal circumstances. But we are in a bind and these aren't 'normal circumstances.' Sometimes that happens and you either get taken a little, or you make more money than you should. It all balances out. Remember that and take the money."

"Yes, ma'am," he said happily. "I'll remember that. And I'll get myself a damn good horse for fifty dollars."

"Do that," Jessie said, "but make sure you feed him better than you fed this one."

20

Arnie flushed with embarrassment. "Yes, ma'am. And we'll bury those two men that you shot before someone comes along and sees them."

"Do you know who they were and who they worked for?" Ki asked.

"Shut your damned yappy mouth!" Milo screamed at his hostler. "You tell 'em and you'll get yourself in deep."

"Never mind," Jessie said. "I'm sure that we'll find out from the Santiagos. And one of them got away."

"He'll bring more," the hostler promised. "Gonna be more blood flowin' over this."

"If there is," Jessie said, "it will be because the cattlemen are forcing it. Sounds to us like they need to learn to live together."

"You can't have both cattle and sheep on the Mogollon Rim or any other damn place," the station tender snapped. "Cattle won't graze where sheep have been."

"That's a myth," Jessie said. "It's just not true."

She turned her back on the man. Ki retrieved their luggage and placed it beside the dead Mexican on the travois. Then they left the three men behind and started off with the dog padding along beside them. It occurred to Jessie that, if they came across more hired gunmen, the only real weapon she had was a pistol in her bags.

No, correct that. She had the samurai and he had all his own deadly weapons. His bow and quiver full of arrows was slung over his shoulder, and in the samurai's hands, they were the equal of a rifle in almost any possible emergency. The samurai could fight with his ancient weapons better than most men could with their new firepower.

"We're buying into real trouble," Ki said as he led the way. "I suspect you know that."

"I do," Jessie replied. "But it sounds to me like it's the

21

kind of trouble that someone needs to buy into and maybe help settle."

The samurai lapsed into silence. One of the things he loved most about Jessica Starbuck was that she never skirted a fight when she believed that injustices were being committed. Not even ones that dealt in bullets and blood.

Chapter 3

Ki stopped so suddenly that the horse bumped into him. Ganso barked and darted into the forest.

"What's the matter?" Jessie asked.

For a moment the samurai stood poised, not a muscle moving. Then he touched his forefinger to his lips and moved away in a low, running crouch that Jessie could never have imitated as he followed the dog into the trees.

Jessie moved around the travois, drew her pistol from her valise, and stepped over beside a pine tree and waited, straining to hear or see something in the forest that surrounded them. She knew full well that the samurai had been alerted to some unforeseen danger. His senses were as refined as those of any Apache, and he was ninja, a man trained in the art of *ninjutsu,* "the ways of the invisible assassin."

Had Ki sensed someone waiting in ambush?

Suddenly Jessie heard a cry of pain and then a low grunt and a gunshot. She jumped up and raced headlong into the forest with a gun in her fist.

"Ki!" she cried.

"It's all right," he said, kneeling down beside the still body of a Mexican boy whose face Ganso was licking. "He must have thought that we were enemies."

Jessie dropped down beside the boy. "Did you use *atemi*?"

"Yes."

Jessie nodded with relief. *Atemi* was the use of pressure points known only to the samurai. By applying pressure to one of the body's pressure points where a large blood vessel could be flattened against bone, Ki could render anyone silently, painlessly unconscious. Jessie had tried to duplicate the act countless times and had never mastered it. But she knew that Ki was a great believer in *atemi,* and this was a good example of its ideal use.

"He must have seen the travois and probably even the dead man," Ki said, picking up an old percussion rifle and examining it.

Jessie also studied the battered rifle. The rifle was as tall as the boy. "He's too young to be trying to defend this ranch."

Ki disarmed the weapon. "He may be too young, but I have a feeling he's a crack shot. Like Juan, he also speaks good English."

"How do you know that?"

"He called me a sonofabitch just before I laid him out," the samurai told her with amusement.

"He can't be more than twelve," Jessie said. "Let's wake him up and make him understand that we mean neither him nor his people any harm."

"He'll be out for only a few minutes," Ki said. "I was light on the touch. Why don't we just load him on the travois and—"

"No!" Jessie said firmly. "Not beside a dead man. Probably a relative."

The samurai conceded that Jessie had a good point. So he settled down to wait, and it was not long before the boy groaned and opened his eyes. The moment he came fully awake, he started violently and tried to jump to his feet, but Jessie and Ki grabbed him before he could scramble out of their grasp.

"Easy," Jessie said. "We mean you no harm."

"You killed Juan!" he cried in anger and took a swing at the samurai, who easily ducked back and then grabbed his wrist.

"I didn't kill him," Ki said. "In fact, this woman and I tried to save him. Was he your brother?"

The boy's eyes filled with tears, and he hugged the black and white dog, who wagged its tail with newfound happiness. "Sí. He was the oldest of us. Juan was eighteen."

"I'm sorry," Jessie said. "He asked that we bring him home for a blessing and a burial. This is what we were doing."

"My name is Pancho Santiago," the boy said in a grave voice as he came to his feet and moved over to the travois. When he saw the dead man's battered face and the horrible rope marks that had turned purple, Pancho's brown eyes filled with fresh tears and he turned away quickly.

"I am sorry," Jessie said.

Pancho drew himself up very straight. "The Santiago men are used to death and pain now," he said. "The gringo gunmen have already killed my father, two brothers, an uncle, and a cousin. There are not many of us left to fight."

"You're too young to be fighting," Jessie said.

But the boy looked her squarely in the eye and answered, "I can kill if I have to. I would gladly give my life to kill Jake Hammer."

"Who is he?"

"He is the man behind the murder of my people," the boy said with growing passion. "He has hired many guns to drive the Mexican people from their land grants. Grants given to our families since the beginning of time!"

"We need you to take us to your rancho," Jessie said. "Maybe there is some way that we can help stop this man."

"No! You are gringo, señorita. It is best that you and your friend give the horse to me and go back. I will see that the animal is returned. You have my word."

But Jessie shook her head. "Juan made us promise to take him back home, and that is what we are going to do."

The boy studied each of them a moment, then he nodded his head. Picking up his old rifle, he stared through the forest.

"I guess we had better follow him," Ki said, grabbing the reins of the horse.

"Yes," Jessie said, wondering what they were getting into.

They came upon the Santiago Rancho at twilight, when the failing sun was kindest to the earth and bathed it in a soft roseate glow. Jessie shielded her eyes and studied the dilapidated adobe home, the sagging roofline of a barn, and the corrals, where a few hundred sheep milled, bleating anxiously.

Three dogs who looked very much like Ganso came bounding up, wagging their tails and barking. Pancho spoke harshly to them and they fell silent.

From out of the big adobe came a collection of old people and children, and then a younger woman who was pregnant. When she saw the travois, she seemed to know what had happened, because she threw back her head and wailed, then fainted and dropped to the ground. The women attended her, but the men came forward slowly until they were close.

Jessie had no difficulty identifying the leader of the Santiago clan. He was of medium height with a hooked nose and long silver hair. His clothes were neat and clean, and he wore a silver ring on each of his index fingers. On either side of him stood two other men his age, and Jessie saw a lot of hard living and grief on their faces.

"Is it Juan?" the leader asked Pancho.

"Sí, Grandfather," the boy said. "He was killed at Butte Station. These people were bringing him back."

"Why?" the man asked in a voice that trembled with pent-up emotion.

Jessie took a deep breath. "Because Juan asked us to bring him back here, and we promised to do it."

The old man drew himself up a little taller. "I thank you and so does my family."

Just then a woman in her fifties stepped forward and moved to the travois. She pulled the canvas back, and when she saw her son, she wept bitterly.

"You must go now," the old man choked.

But Jessie pretended not to hear. "Two of the three men who killed Juan are dead and the other is wounded," she said. "I thought you should know."

The old man looked at the samurai. "You killed them?"

Ki nodded. "We both did."

The Mexican's head swiveled and his eyes looked deep into Jessie's. "You can use a gun?"

"Yes."

He lifted his arm and pointed toward a pine tree about a hundred yards away. "Shoot it, please."

Jessie's gun was now strapped around her waist. She drew and fired in one smooth but unhurried motion, and as the gun bucked in her fist, they all saw the bark splinter off

27

the tree leaving a single white spot about as big as the palm of a man's hand.

"I am not as fast as a professional or as accurate as Annie Oakley or a Wild West Show performer," she said, reloading the weapon as everyone looked on in amazement. "But I am able to protect myself."

"My name is Antonio Escobar Lopez Santiago," the man said with great respect. "This is a sad day for us, but you are welcome to remain here as long as you wish."

Jessie nodded and introduced herself and the samurai. Then they set about to untie poor Juan from the travois.

"He was roped and dragged," Jessie explained once. "But he died bravely."

The muscles around Antonio's eyes tightened and he said. "We will make them pay for this! We will take blood for blood this time."

"No!" a woman said as she stepped forward. "I am his mother. There has been enough killing."

But Antonio's face grew dark with anger. "The killing will not stop until Hammer is dead and so are his friends. They will not let us live in peace, Maria! You must understand this before we are all slaughtered like our sheep!"

Maria turned away quickly and began to cry. Jessie stood helplessly by, and then she moved over to the horse and unloosened its cinch. She was going to stay awhile longer unless these people demanded that she and Ki go away.

There was no priest, but early the next morning a religious service was held, and the women wore mantillas and the men white shirts and ties. Holding flickering candles, the Santiago clan sang and marched as they carried Juan up to a small knoll, where they buried him with a few simple but moving words of prayer. When the burial was over, Jessie waited quietly until she saw that Antonio was alone, then she went to speak privately with him. "Señor Santiago, could we walk over by that stream and speak together?"

The old man nodded and followed her.

In her customary fashion Jessie got right to the point. "I would like to know more about this man named Jake Hammer and how many families like yours there are in these mountains fighting against him."

"There are three families," the old man said. "Ours has the most land. Twenty-two thousand acres given to my grandfather by the Spanish governor of this land many, many years ago. The Escobar family's grant is next to ours and has seventeen thousand, and the Lopez grant is the smallest, but their land has the most grass and water. They have suffered most. There is also a man named Señor Ben Rodgers. He has lost many sheep and two sheeptenders. He was shot three days ago, but we found him and have taken him to a hiding place where he is recovering."

"So," Jessie said. "It is the sheep that this man named Hammer and his friends hate so much."

"Yes," Antonio said. "And Mexicans. But Señor Rodgers, he is white like you and he is on our side. He has sworn to kill Jake Hammer, but I do not think he can do it unless Hammer was stupid enough to go onto Rodgers's land."

"How many other cattle ranchers have formed against you?"

"I do not know. Three or four cattlemen? Maybe more. They want our land and water," Antonio said bitterly. "They shoot us from the trees, and they have raided our camps, killed our dogs, and then burned our sheep. They have driven them off the high mesas and poisoned our water holes."

"Have you tried asking the law for help?"

The old man spat at the ground. "There is only 'Colt's Law,' as they call it."

"But there has to be a federal marshal and a court of law somewhere that has jurisdiction over this part of the country."

"I do not know what this word *jurisdiction* means," he said.

"It means that someone has to have control, be in a position of authority to uphold the law in this country."

"The marshal's name is Buck Timberman. He is a friend of Jake Hammer and the other cattle ranchers. He is a bad man, señorita. He killed one of my sons three years ago."

Antonio's weathered brown face twisted up with pain. "We found Adolpho hanging from a rope. It was the damned marshal!"

Jessie looked to Ki and the samurai said, "Where is this sheriff?"

"He is in Alpine," the old sheepman said.

"And the judge?"

"Same place. It is the county seat."

Ki and Jessie had stopped at Alpine the day before. It was the largest town in the area, and now that Antonio had mentioned it, she had seen a county courthouse and sheriff's office.

"I think," Jessie said slowly, "that we had better pay them a visit."

"Ask the sheriff if he has seen Mando. Ask him if Mando is still alive."

"He is . . . ?"

"He is another of my grandsons," Antonio said. "He is the best fighter left among us now. If he can, he will return and help us kill Jake Hammer."

"I see." Jessie took a deep breath. "Maybe we can help

30

you. If the law is bad in Alpine, we will fight to get a new marshal."

"You could not do that," the old man said. "The marshal and the judge are powerful men. They take money from Jake Hammer and his friends. They would kill you, too, before they would agree to letting us keep our land grants."

"We do not kill easily," Jessie said. "Many have tried."

Antonio thought about this for several moments and then he said, "Who are you and why do you want to help us?"

"We are from Texas. I own a cattle ranch there, but I have no hatred of sheep and sheepmen. In fact, I think it wise that both are owned so that ranchers do not fall prey to so many bad years of low prices."

Antonio's smile was painful to see. "Haven't you heard? Cattle will not graze where sheep have been."

"I know that is not true," Jessie said. "What is true is that sheep crop the ground very close and sometimes even pull grass up by the roots. But if it is not overgrazed by them and the grass is given a few weeks to grow up again, then the cattle will eat it."

"This is so," Antonio said. "I have seen this many times, but the cattlemen have never seen it even once. They do not *want* to see it."

"Then we will make them see it anyway," Jessie said. "And I will find this Mando for you if he is alive."

"I think he is alive," Antonio said. "We sent him away to find a gunfighter."

"But why?"

"We gave him one hundred American dollars to find someone to teach him how to draw and fire the gun. Like you just did, señorita! We need a . . . how do you say it? A *pistolero*."

"You want a professional gunfighter."

31

"Yes," the old man said, bobbing his head up and down. "That is what you call it. A professional gunfighter."

"Your Mando, he is quick and brave?"

"Very," Antonio said. "Once, as a boy, he even fought a cougar with nothing but a stick. He has the scars to prove his courage."

"How will we know him if we see him?" Ki asked.

"He is tall and handsome," Antonio said. "If you see him, he will be wearing a silver ring like this."

The old man held up his hand so that Jessie and Ki could get a closer look. The ring was silver and turquoise with a piece of red coral rock shaped like a heart. It was a very unusual ring, and Jessie knew she would recognize it in a moment.

"I will remember it," she said. "I would also like to see this Ben Rodgers. Perhaps he needs the care of a doctor."

"He would not accept it," Antonio said.

"Why not?"

"He is a . . . how do you say it? A mountain man. He believes in the cures of the Indians, and even we had great difficulty helping him. He is very stubborn, that one."

"Well, where is he?"

"He has a ranch to the north of us, but he has no home. His home is the forest and the meadow. His sheep are few and he has fierce dogs that will attack his enemies on command."

"Does he live alone in the forest?"

"Yes," Antonio said. "With his dogs and his sheep. I do not think he likes people very much."

"It sounds as if he has little reason to like them," Jessie said. "Where can we find him?"

"If you go onto his ranch to the north, he will find you," Antonio promised. "Yesterday, when we went to take him food, he was gone. No one will find him now."

Jessie turned to Ki. "Maybe you had better find him. Tell the man that we are going to help him keep his land."

Antonio shook his head. "Señorita," he said in gentle protest. "You do not understand. This man Rodgers, he would not want your help. He only wants to be left alone."

Jessie figured she knew the type. Men like Ben Rodgers were hermits and sometimes half crazy from the loneliness they endured. Often, they had been hurt by people and were suspicious and distrustful of anyone.

"All right," Jessie said. "But it seems to me that the sheepmen in this country ought to band together and fight. Standing alone, you have no chance."

Antonio shrugged his shoulders. "When they come, we fight. If we go to fight them, then we will become outlaws and be hunted down and hanged. The judge and the marshal, they are all against us. So what can we do?"

"That's what we are going to Alpine to find out," Jessie said. "Can I buy horses and saddles from you?"

"You already have one horse," Antonio said.

"I want to buy *good* horses," Jessie told him. "And I will pay you fairly."

"We have good horses, but you do not need to pay anything. Just find Mando. Tell him that he must come to help us now. Tell him that they killed Juan. That will bring him home . . . if he still lives."

"I will try to see that your legal rights and those of the other sheep ranchers are protected," Jessie said. "You are not the only sheep-raising families that have been persecuted by cattle ranchers. The same thing has happened in Wyoming, Montana, and Colorado."

"We are few, the cattlemen are many," Antonio said. "Last month they drove a thousand head of my sheep over the cliffs. Only a miracle saved Pancho from also being pushed over the cliff to his death."

33

"The rimrocking will stop," Jessie vowed.

"You mean well," Antonio said. "But you do not understand what we are up against. Yesterday, you killed two of our enemies. Hammer and his friends will hire two more and two more until he wins."

"If I have to," Jessie said, "I can also hire men."

"Who would fight for Mexicans against whites?"

"It is that but more," Jessie reminded him. "Ben Rodgers is a white man. This is about cattle and sheep and greed. It is about men who have taken control of the law and are using it to take what belongs to others."

"I will get the horses for you," Antonio said as he walked away. His action said louder than words that, while he appreciated her sentiments, he doubted her and the samurai would live long enough to see them put into action.

★

Chapter 4

When Jessie and Ki rode into Alpine, the first thing they saw was a large crowd moving toward the courthouse building, and it was clear that the citizens of this county seat were riled up about something.

"What's all the excitement about?" Jessie asked as they overtook a man walking on crutches and trying to keep up with the pack.

"There's gonna be a murder trial and a hanging is what the excitement is all about!" the man exclaimed, puffing noisily and filled with excitement. "A damn greaser shot down two men over at Rosie's Place last Saturday night. Shot 'em down in cold blood, and Judge Larson, he's gonna sentence that murderin' Mexican to the gallows for sure. That Mexican, he ain't nothin' but a sheep-lovin' sonofabitch!"

Jessie glanced at Ki, then back to the man. "What's his name?"

"His name!" the man cried. "Why, it's Mando Santiago. That whole damn family of greasers is a pack of varmits."

Jessie's face clouded and she spurred her horse onward.

When they reached the courthouse, she and Ki dismounted and quickly tied their animals, then pushed their way inside, where a standing-room-only crowd waited impatiently for the trial to begin.

Jessie surveyed the grim-faced jury, and it was obvious at a glance that there was not a Mexican, a sheepman, or a friendly face among the bunch. She had no trouble identifying the sheriff as a tall, broad-shouldered man in his early fifties.

Sheriff Timberman's badge was polished and the tips of his mustache were waxed. He'd obviously been a fine physical specimen of manhood in his youth, but now his face was blotchy from too much drinking and his nose was red and bulbous. He had a small potbelly that pushed over his cartridge belt. Despite that, Buck Timberman still had the look of a bad man to cross. He still had a lot of power in his arms and shoulders, and his lantern-jaw and big fists gave him the look of a man who enjoyed a fight.

"All right everybody!" Timberman bellowed. "I want order in this courtroom! This ain't no damn carnival. It's a court of law, and you'll all show some respect for the law, or me and my deputies will throw you out the damn door!"

The crowd grumbled and didn't like being talked to that way, but Timberman glared them into a resentful silence except for a very well-dressed man in a tailored suit who yelled, "Take it easy, Buck! You know the judge is going to hang the greaser whether or not we're quiet."

"Yeah, I know that as well as you," Timberman said. "But I still reckon we'll have some respect for the law, Mr. Hammer."

Both Jessie and Ki took a closer look at Jake Hammer. He was a man of average size wearing expensive clothes, a gold watch and chain, and a big diamond ring. Despite his attempt at joviality, Jessie could see a hardness around his

36

eyes. He was younger than she had expected for a man of so much power and influence, probably no more than thirty-five, and there were several tough-looking men around him.

"Hearye, hearye!" the baliff called. "Everybody on your feet. Court is now in session with the Honorable Judge Lawrence P. Larson presiding."

The judge was a small, ferret-faced man with stern features and thick bifocals. He was dressed in a black robe, and when he took his seat, he cleared his throat without looking up at the crowd and snapped, "Baliff, bring the accused prisoner into the courtroom at once!"

"Yes, sir, Your Honor," the bailiff said, disappearing along with the sheriff and a deputy.

Everyone in the room heard a scuffle and then a curse which was immediately followed by the sound of a body striking the floor. A moment later Timberman and his deputy dragged Mando Santiago into the courtroom.

Mando was dazed and had to be supported to his chair, where he was quickly handcuffed. His head rolled back and everyone saw that his face was marred by a beating. A beating so severe that his features were unrecognizable. One of his eyes was completely swollen shut, and his lips had been broken by someone's fist. He was bleeding from the mouth again, probably the result of the blows that he had just received before being hauled into the courtroom. Jessie clenched her fists in silent anger. It was obvious that the man had been mistreated.

Judge Larson banged his gavel. "Mr. Burt, let's hear testimony from the first witness."

"Yes, sir, Your Honor," an attorney said as he motioned for a cowboy to take the stand.

"This is Mr. Chick Hunsley."

"Swear him in," the judge ordered his bailiff.

Hunsley was sworn in and he took the witness stand.

"Go ahead and tell it in your own words," the attorney prompted. "Don't leave anything out."

Hunsley was tall, young, and nervous. He licked his lips and pointed an accusing finger at Mando. "That Mexican, he was with Miss Ginger Brown last night. Ginger is the prettiest whore in town, as anybody with eyes knows."

Lawson cleared his throat and said to the attorney, "Have the witness stick to the facts of the case. Miss Brown's occupation and appearance are not an issue in this case."

"Yes, sir," the attorney said. "Keep to the facts, Mr. Hunsley."

"Well, sure," the cowboy said, shifting in the hard witness chair. "Anyway, Mando Santiago, he was in her room so long that me and Dave and John, we started pounding on the door. We'd paid to see Ginger, not some other woman."

"All three of you?" the judge asked.

"Well, not at the same time," Hunsley said, amid the snickers of the crowd.

"Go on," the attorney said. "What happened after you started knocking on the door?"

Hunsley swallowed. "We didn't know Ginger was with no greaser. Hell, if we had, we'd have kept our money!"

More laughter. The judge banged his gavel down on the bench until the court grew quiet, and he said in a stern voice, "This is not the time or the place for levity! If you people can't be silent, then I'll have you run the hell out of my courtroom."

Jessie leaned close to Ki. "Mando doesn't even have an attorney to defend him," she whispered. "This trial is a farce!"

Hunsley droned on. "Well, the next thing I knew, the

38

door was flying open and there was that greaser sonofabitch standing in his longjohns with a gun in his fist and it was leveled right at us."

"And what did you do?" the attorney asked.

"I decided right sudden that it might be healthier to find me another whore," the cowboy said. "So I just backed on down the hallway, and I thought that Dave and John would do the same. And I guess they did."

"What do you mean, 'you guess they did?'" the attorney questioned. "You did see what happened, didn't you?"

Jake Hammer cleared his throat loudly. Hunsley's eyes sought him out, then he nodded his head vigorously at the judge and jury. "Oh, yes sir! I saw everything. The Mexican there, he was wild and actin' crazy. He started cussin' and swearin'. Sayin' things that would scorch a man's ears, and then he opened fire with his sixgun. Mando Santiago shot Dave and John down without giving them a chance."

The courtroom exploded with fury and someone yelled, "I say we don't waste any more time. Let's just hang him now!"

But Timberman drew his sixgun and raised it over his head, then shouted, "This is a court of law. Santiago hasn't been sentenced to hang yet, and until he is, there will be no necktie party in Alpine. Not as long as I'm the marshal."

The judge banged his gavel down again and again until the courtroom fell silent, and the judge stood up and shook his gavel at them all. "One more outburst and I will instruct the marshal and his deputies to empty the courtroom. Sentencing has not taken place, and until it has been, I will not tolerate these interruptions."

The judge turned to Mando. "Mr. Santiago, I can see that you are unfit to speak in your own behalf, therefore . . ."

"I'll speak," he said in a choking voice that riveted the courtroom's attention to him. "I demand to be heard!"

"You don't demand any damned thing!" Timberman swore, moving over to him with his fists balled.

"Don't you dare hit him again!" Jessie shouted.

Now everyone turned to look at her and Ki.

"Who the devil are you!" Timberman demanded.

Jessie had not really intended to speak. In fact, she wished she hadn't. But her cry had come unbidden, and now that she had grabbed center stage, it was impossible to back down. "My name is Miss Jessica Starbuck."

"And what the hell do you have to say about anything going on here?" Timberman demanded.

"I speak as an American who understands the basic rights of every citizen. Rights like being innocent until proven guilty! This isn't a trial, this is a mockery of justice!"

Judge Lawson banged his gavel down hard, and his face burned scarlet. "You are in contempt of court. I hereby fine you one hundred dollars!"

"I'll gladly pay it if you promise to conduct yourself like a judge sworn to uphold justice. And if you don't, I'll take this matter directly to Governor Benson Billings and see that there is an immediate and full investigation into this matter."

"Sheriff Timberman!" the judge raged. "I want that woman apprehended and placed under custody in jail!"

Timberman blinked. "Now, Judge, you know that my jail ain't got but one cell, and it's being used by Santiago. I—"

"I order you to arrest and lock her up!"

Timberman shrugged his big shoulders and started for Jessie. Ki stepped in front of her, but Jessie said, "No, it's

40

all right. Telegraph the governor and tell him what what has happened here."

"Do you know him?" Ki whispered.

"Actually," Jessie admitted under her breath, "I don't. Better get word to the governor of Texas and have him make the contact."

"But that could take days!"

"Maybe my being in jail is the only thing that will keep Mando alive until we can get to the bottom of things," she said in a rush. "It's all I could think of to do."

"Miss Starbuck," Timberman rumbled, "you heard Judge Lawson. I got to arrest you. If you'd have kept your damn mouth shut, you wouldn't be in this mess."

When he grabbed her arm his fingers bit into her flesh and it hurt. Jessie stiffled a cry of pain, but Ki saw it in her eyes. He grabbed the sheriff's forearm and his thumb dug into the big man's flesh, hitting a nerve and causing Timberman to stiffen, then reach for his gun, and he swore, "You want some of this trouble too, huh!"

Ki was about to strike when suddenly Jake Hammer pushed in between them and said, "Sheriff, before this gets out of control, why don't you just arrest Miss Starbuck and leave it be at that."

Timberman, who was a good four inches taller than the samurai and fifty pounds heavier, was reluctant to let it pass, but the cattle baron's hard tone and clipped words could not be ignored. "Sure," he said, "whatever you say, Mr. Hammer."

He pulled on Jessie's arm and said, "Come on!"

"Timberman!"

The sheriff was pulled up short by Hammer's voice. He turned. "Yes, sir?"

"This is a prominent Texas cattle rancher and a real lady," Hammer said. "Not a drunken whore you're arrest-

41

ing. Now you treat her gently and with respect, or you'll hear from me. Is that understood?"

Timberman's beefy face darkened, but he still managed to nod his head, then call for one of his deputies to take Jessie away.

"I'll be all right," she said to the samurai. "You stay and listen to this trial. I want to know everything Mando says. And I want to know the verdict."

Ki nodded, but he wasn't a bit happy. "You'll be out soon," he promised.

"Of course she will," Hammer said. "I think the judge has overreacted here, and during the first recess I'll speak to him personally."

He touched Jessie's arm. "No need to be contacting the governor of this territory or of the state of Texas, Miss Starbuck. I'm aware of who you are, and I'll see that this little misunderstanding is taken care of right away. We damn sure aren't going to put you in the same jail with a murdering Mexican."

Jessie shot a cold glance at the suave cattleman as she was hauled away.

It took several minutes before the trial was resumed, and during that time, Ki saw Jake Hammer manage to get a private word in with the judge. He couldn't tell what was said, but the judge did give him a hard look before he cleared his throat.

"We'll have a fifteen-minute recess and then we'll continue. But I warn everyone, I'll have you all jailed just as quick as that young woman if you insult this court or refuse to hold your silence."

Ki pushed outside the courtroom to get a breath of fresh air. He watched as a deputy led Jessie into the jail and then closed the door. Things had not gotten off to a very good start here in Alpine. Not good at all. And unless he was badly mistaken, this trial would be over before the day, and Mando Santiago would be sentenced to hang by the neck until dead.

When the trial resumed, Mando Santiago had recovered enough to take the witness stand. Since his testimony wasn't going to be considered anyway, Ki noticed that the judge did not even bother to ask the bailiff to swear him in.

Mando noticed it, too, because he snatched a Bible off the table it was resting upon and said, "I hereby swear to tell the whole truth and nothing but the truth, so help me God."

The judge was steaming, and he shot a murderous glance at both the sheriff and the bailiff, but growled, "Sit down, Santiago. Let's hear your version, but make it brief."

Mando had kept his head down, but now he raised it and stared with his one undamaged eye directly at the audience, which took a collective gasp because the sight was so shocking. Mando had been a very handsome man before the beating, but he might never be again, even if he lived.

Through broken lips Mando spoke clearly and loud enough for everyone to hear him. "I was with Miss Ginger . . . when men began to pound on the door. I yelled for them to go away. To come back later. But they were drunk and would not listen. When they kept beating on the door, I put on my gun and went to chase them away."

"That's a bald-faced lie!" Chick Hunsley shouted, coming to his feet. "You gonna believe a damn greaser over a white man?"

The judge banged his gavel down hard. "Sit down, Mr. Hunsley. You had your turn."

Ki noticed that the judge had looked to Jake Hammer, and now Hammer was nodding with approval. It was painfully obvious that Hammer was in control of both the judge and the sheriff.

"Continue with your testimony," the judge said.

Mando shook his head as if to clear it of some inner pain that Ki had no trouble imagining was the result of his beating. "Sure I had my gun out when I opened the hotel room door. Anybody would. But I never figured I'd meet up with men stupid enough to draw on a man with a gun pointed at them."

"I find that very damn difficult to believe," the judge said, glancing at the jury, most of whom nodded in full agreement. "That just doesn't ring true."

"But it is true!" Mando shouted. "They were drunk and when they saw I was a half-breed, they went crazy. I yelled at them in warning, but they wouldn't listen. I pistol-whipped Chick and knocked him down. You can see that knot on the side of his head. I gave him that and it saved his life. I'd have pistol-whipped all three if there had been time. But there wasn't. So I fired in self-defense."

"He's lying, Judge!" Hunsley cried. "Why, it was murder!"

"Is that all you have to say in your own defense?" the judge asked.

"No!" Mando said hotly. "Everyone knows I've been gone, and they remember what I promised to do when I returned. I swore vengeance on Jake Hammer and his kind, and so they came after me. This whole thing was a setup from beginning to end."

"I think we've heard enough," the judge said in a voice that dripped with sarcasm. He looked to the jury. "Do you need to retire to reach a verdict?"

The jury shook its head.

"Wait a minute!" Ki shouted. "What about Miss Ginger Brown! She was there. Shouldn't she be called to testify?"

"She left town suddenly!" Buck Timberman shouted. "Anyway, what the hell business is this of yours! You want to go to jail, too?"

Ki did not want to go to jail. If both he and Jessie were incarcerated, they'd be of little use to anyone. So he shook his head.

"Then keep your damn yellow trap shut!" Timberman barked.

Ki ground his teeth in silence, aware of the hostility that was being directed his way by the citizens.

But he knew one thing for sure. He was going to find and have a talk with this Miss Ginger Brown—if she was still in any condition to talk. And he'd do it right away.

The judge rapped his gavel sharply on the bench and said, "We've heard the testimony of Mr. Hunsley and of the accused. If the jury is ready to announce its verdict, then you may do so."

A tall cadaverous man leaned over, and the jury consulted among itself for a moment, then the man stood up with his hat in his bony fists and said, "Your Honor, this is a cut and dried case of double murder. Pure and simple it is. We find the defendant guilty of murder in the first degree."

The judge smiled. The courtroom burst into applause as the judge banged his gavel down hard. Buck Timberman hauled Mando to his feet to receive his death sentence, and the courtroom fell into silent expectation. This was the moment they had been waiting for.

"Mando Santiago," the judge intoned, not even looking at the man. "You heard the verdict. I have no choice but to sentence you to—"

"Your Honor!" Jake Hammer interrupted loudly. "May I say something? In light of the fact that the only witness that could have supported Mando's testimony has suddenly vanished, it does cast a . . . a question on things. In light of that, I think that a sentence of life in prison would be fairer than a hanging."

"No!" Mando roared, throwing his head back and raising his manacles in anger. "I would rather die than spend my life behind bars!"

Hammer smiled cruelly and met the judge's eye. "Judge, wouldn't you agree that we ought to show Mando Santiago a little mercy? No sense in having someone from outside telling us that we didn't show the convicted killer a little clemency. Don't you agree?"

Ki shook his head. Hammer was smart. He knew that Jessie had connections with men in high places, and now he'd robbed Jessie of her ammunition. Robbed the situation of its explosiveness and urgency.

The judge understood, too. He nodded. "Yes," he said, almost cheerfully. "I believe you might have a very good point, Mr. Hammer. Yes, I do! And I applaud your citizen's contribution to justice."

He looked down on Mando. "Mando Santiago," he droned, "I hereby order you to be taken on the next stage to Yuma, where you will be incarcerated at the territorial prison for the rest of your natural life."

Mando lunged at the judge. He actually managed to grab his sleeve before Buck Timberman brought the barrel of his Colt smashing down on his skull, dropping him like a shot buck.

Ki swore silently as everyone began to shout and grin, congratulating each other as if they had themselves won some sort of victory.

"Your name is Ki and you're a samurai, aren't you," Hammer said, coming to stand before him.

"That's right."

"I've read about you," Hammer said. "I've read that

46

you use strange weapons and that you fight with your feet as well as your hands. I read an interview on Miss Jessica Starbuck once, and you received a fair amount of ink. The reporter who wrote the piece claimed that you can do all sorts of amazing things with funny weapons."

Ki started to walk away, but one of Hammer's gunmen blocked his path and said, "Mr. Hammer is talking to you. Better be polite and listen."

Ki said to Hammer. "Get him out of my way or I'll break his arms."

"Step aside, Ed."

Ed reluctantly stepped aside.

"Ki, I'm going to spring Miss Starbuck from our jail. I don't want her to be around a scum like Mando Santiago. And when she is free, I hope you are smart enough to convince her that it would be much healthier in Texas."

"I let Miss Starbuck make the decisions," Ki said. "And I think she's decided to stay and fix some injustices in this part of the country. Seems to me that the sheepmen are being killed or run off this range."

"They're nothing but a bunch of sheep-loving greasers," Hammer said. "But then, that probably is in their favor in your estimation, seeing as how you're half Japanese yourself."

Ki started to leave and Hammer said, "Maybe I should let Miss Starbuck stay in the same cell with that Mexican murderer. Be a shame what could happen to her, and it sure would ruin a lady's reputation, but I guess some women need to learn things the hard way."

Ki's blood ran cold. "Mr. Hammer," he said, turning to look deep into the cattleman's eyes. "You just do whatever you have in mind to do—because we will. And things are going to change around here."

Hammer's smile slipped a little. "You're out of your

element on the Mogollon Rim. Too bad you can't figure that out for yourselves before things get real nasty."

Even a samurai has his limits of self control, and because Ki was fast approaching his, he turned and walked out of the courtroom. He would see Jessie and tell her what had happened here, and then he'd wire the governor of Texas or maybe even a few United States congressmen before he found out what had happened to Ginger Brown.

This country might be dominated by the cattlemen, but men like Jake Hammer, Judge Larson, and Buck Timberman had better learn that this was Arizona, not their own little kingdom where their rule was law.

Chapter 5

Jessie winced when the heavy iron door slammed shut, locking her and Mando Santiago in the dirty jail cell.

"Woman," Sheriff Buck Timberman snapped, "you brought this grief upon yourself. You had every chance to get out of Alpine and save yourself this trouble, but you wouldn't listen."

Jessie looked around the cell. At least ten cockroaches scuttered about the filthy floor. "Sheriff," she said, "I want a broom and some soap and water. There's nothing I can do about your pigsty of a jailhouse, but I can at least clean this cell. And I want a doctor sent over here immediately."

Timberman's bushy eyebrows shot up. "Clean the cell! Jeezus! If that ain't just like some damn fancy woman! And as for a doctor, save your money. Mando ain't going to need any fixin' up in the Yuma Prison. They're all ugly over there anyway!"

The big sheriff grinned maliciously and turned on his heel, but he did go over and get a broom and dustpan, then sent his deputy to get the doctor.

Jessie sat down on a bunk without a mattress and studied Mando. He looked so beaten and forlorn that she hesitated to say what had to be said. "I came from your rancho," she said gently. "I'm afraid I have more bad news."

He stiffened as if he expected another physical blow. "My mother, is she . . ."

"She's fine," Jessie said quickly. "But I'm very sorry to say that Juan is dead."

Mando groaned and covered his face as Jessie told him what had happened and then how she and Ki had taken the young man's body to be buried in the family cemetery.

"I thank you for your kindness to me and to my family," Mando said quietly. "But I think that you are foolish for getting into such trouble for us. If you and your friend killed two of Jake Hammer's gunmen, you are lucky to still be alive. Maybe your friend would also be safer in this jail."

"Ki is a samurai."

"A what?"

"I'll explain it to you some other time," she said. "But he understands danger and can take care of himself."

"What about you?" Mando asked. "This jail is no place for a woman."

"I won't be kept here for very long. Ki will be working on that right away. And as for getting involved in what's going on in this country, well, I have no regrets."

"Maybe that is because you do not yet understand what is going on."

"Your grandfather told me about the rimrocking and the murders. I understand what your people are up against."

"It is not just my people," Mando said. "It is anyone who runs sheep in this country."

"I like this country and I was thinking of buying a piece of it."

50

"It is better sheep than cattle country," Mando said. "And you are not a sheepwoman."

"I'm a *businesswoman*," she told him quietly as she took the dustpan from the sheriff and then began to sweep the floor. "And a champion of the underdog when I see grave injustice."

Sheriff Timberman returned with an old broom. "Here," he said, sticking it through the bars. "And honey, how about sweeping out the whole office when you finish in there. Hell, if you do a real good job, I might even give you a little reward."

When Timberman bumped his hips suggestively at Jessie, Mando leapt at the bars and gripped them until his knuckles were white. "You swine! Come in here with just your fists and I'll teach you some manners."

Timberman started to unbuckle his gunbelt. He was coming into the cell, and he was going to administer another beating to Mando.

"Do that," Jessie warned "and I'll see you never wear a badge again. This man is in no condition to fight, and you're an officer of the law."

Timberman hesitated, then cinched up his gunbelt again. "Woman," he said, "you might be a big deal in Texas, but in this neck of the woods, you're nothing but a pain in the ass. Now I'm going out to get myself something to eat, but there will be a deputy sitting outside, and there'd best not be any more trouble from you. Mando, if you want a woman, this will be your last damn chance and you'd better take it."

Mando colored with embarrassment, and Timberman, seeing his discomfort, snickered with derision. "Hell, Mando. I reckon the only thing you know how to poke are whores and ewes!"

With an obscene laugh, Timberman slammed the door

51

behind himself and left them alone for a few minutes.

"Nice man," Jessie said. "He been the sheriff here very long?"

"About as long as I can remember," Mando replied, still too embarrassed to look at her. "He and the judge have been running things for the Hammers ever since I was a kid. It used to be Jake's father, Seth Hammer. Then the old man died and Jake took over. One is as bad as the other."

Mando looked bleak. "I was supposed to come back and clean them out," he said quietly. "My family counted on me to come back a big *pistolero*. Instead, I get caught with a woman and look at what has happened to me now."

Jessie managed a thin smile. "Things will get better. I promise that time is on our side. You won't be in Yuma Prison long before I raise such a stink that there will be an investigation. That wasn't a trial you had a few minutes ago, and when I tell the governor of this territory what happened, there will be another trial and you'll be released, or at least have the sentence sharply reduced. The key is Ginger Brown. She's the only one that can back up your testimony."

"They probably killed her," Mando said in anger. "Or at least they will now for sure."

"Then Ki will have to find her and save her," Jessie told him. "Any idea where she might be found?"

"No," Mando said. "If she's still alive, then I suppose they've got her hidden someplace."

"Maybe she was smart enough to run," Jessie offered.

Mando nodded. "That's possible. Ginger is smart. She'd see the handwriting and how things would shape up for her. Yeah, she might have gotten away, but it wouldn't have been easy. The stage hasn't been through since I shot those two Hammer gunnies that pounded on my hotel room door."

52

"Then if they didn't have her, she's either hiding in Alpine or she's gotten a horse and made her escape."

"She was a pretty fair horsewoman," Mando said. "Ginger could do most anything she set her mind to. If she got out of that hotel and started running, she'd give them a merry chase."

At just that moment the front door opened and a rumpled old man with a black medical bag entered with Ki on his heels and a deputy close behind them.

"Open the cell, deputy," the doctor growled. "I can't treat an injury through the bars."

The deputy wasn't too pleased by the arrangement. "If anyone tries anything funny," he said, drawing his gun, "I'll kill the damn bunch of you, and I'll be within my rights stopping a jail break."

"Open the door," the doctor repeated. 'No one is stupid enough to try and make an escape in the middle of the day with half the town outside watching."

The door was opened and the doctor came inside. "Mando," he said, "take off that shirt and let's have a look at the damages. And by the way, I was sorry to hear about Juan. He was a fine young man."

Mando dipped his chin in agreement and removed his shirt. Even Ki, accustomed to seeing bruises and injuries, was somewhat shocked by the damage inflicted on Mando's lean and muscular body. It was covered with bruises and dried blood. He looked as if he'd been beaten with a club from his shoulders down to his waist.

The doctor gently touched the contusions, all the while shaking his head with disgust and anger. "Whoever did this was real thorough. He knew what he was doing and he didn't miss a lick, did he."

"No," Mando said quietly. "Buck Timberman has had a lot of practice beating the hell out of Mexican sheepmen."

"Yeah, but I remember the time he tackled big Ben Rodgers here on our main street. That's one sheepman he'll never take on again. Rodgers almost knocked his brains out before they dragged him off. I wish Ben would have killed him. We'd all be better off today."

"You better shut your damn mouth!" the deputy swore. "Buck ain't gonna like the way you're sidin' with these folks, Doc!"

The doctor said, "Hell, Buck knows what I think about him. He knows I owe him half my yearly income. Without Buck shooting up and beating the hell out of folks, I'd have starved out a long time ago."

The deputy did not know what to say, and his mouth crimped down at the corners. In disapproving silence he stood off to one side of the office and glared while the doctor finished his examination.

"No ribs broken," the doctor said. "Some loose teeth, and I can't say how soon the swelling in your eye will go down. Might take a month before it looks right again."

"In the Yuma Prison," Mando said, "it won't matter. I hear the prisoners over there are put in earthen cells dug back under the riverbank."

"Yeah," the doctor said cryptically. "We lock up men in cells that we wouldn't use to confine dogs or pigs."

The doctor opened his bag and pulled out a bottle of black syrup. "It's liniment," he said. "Works on horses same as humans. The stuff is a derivitive of coal tar and it smells awful, but it seems to pull the blood out to the flesh and take down the swelling and discoloration. You're going to be feeling a whole lot better in a few days, Mando. I just wish you were going home instead of to prison."

"Thanks, Doc," Mando said. "I'd pay you, but I don't have any money. Timberman took it all and . . ."

"Never mind," the doctor said. "Juan used to run errands for me when he was small. I liked that kid. He deserved a better fate."

"Doc," the deputy called, "you're diggin' your own damn grave with that kind of talk. If I was you, I'd remember who runs this town and who's your bread and butter."

The doctor spun around. "It isn't Jake Hammer," he snapped. "His men never seem to get hurt, except for the one that I treated for a gunshot wound yesterday. Said his gun went off by accident. But I sort of had my suspicions."

Ki stepped forward. "Where is the man, Doc? I'd like to have a word with him about Juan Santiago."

The deputy came charging over to the cell. "Doc! You shut up or you'll wind up in a pine box!"

The doctor was so upset he would have defied the deputy, but Jessie said, "Never mind, Doc. It's not worth risking your life or practice to find that man. I have a feeling there will be plenty of others who will be needing your services. Who knows? They might all be Hammer men. Deputy, you might even be the first of them."

Jessie had meant to incense the deputy, and she hadn't failed.

"Lady, you're gonna leave this town in a box yourself."

He advanced toward the cell. "And you, mister. You'd better just keep your nose clean or we'll have you in jail, too."

Muscles bunched under Ki's shirt at the threat.

"Ki, no," Jessie said softly. "You understand what has to be done."

The samurai pulled his eyes away from the deputy with some reluctance. "I'll be around," he said. "And deputy, if you or the marshal allow anything to happen to Miss Starbuck, you'll both die."

55

The deputy started to make some abrasive comment, but Ki's hand settled on his shoulder and the samurai's fingers dug into his flesh so powerfully that the man lifted up onto the balls of his feet.

Ki released him and stepped back. The deputy did not reach for his gun. His eyes reflected pain and astonishment, and he sagged weakly against the bars. "You better get out of here now," he managed to whisper.

Ki left without a backward glance. He went straight to the telegraph office and sent a message to the governor of Texas with this simple message: MISS STARBUCK WRONGFULLY DETAINED IN ALPINE, ARIZONA JAIL. HELP APPRECIATED, KI.

The telegraph operator studied the message. "Mr. Ki," he said, "I don't know if I dare send this. If Buck Timberman finds out . . ."

"He won't need to find out unless you tell him," Ki said. "So send it as written. And do it now."

The telegraph operator nodded worriedly. "Just remember that I just did my job. Nothing more. Just my job."

"It's too bad that the law doesn't do its job as well," Ki said, hearing the telegraph keys begin to clatter. "It sure would make things a lot simpler around here."

Chapter 6

Just before he left the telegraph office, Ki turned around at the door and said to the operator, "Say, mister. You don't know where I can find Miss Ginger Brown, do you?"

The telegraph operator snorted. "I was at Mando Santiago's trial, and there's no grass growin' between my ears, stranger. Even if you found somebody that knew where she was, they'd have to be mighty stupid to admit the fact to you."

"That's what I figured you'd say," Ki answered. "Can you at least point me in the general direction of Rosie's Place, where Miss Brown last worked?"

"Humph!" the man snorted a second time. "Good riddance, I say!"

Ki headed down the street, and when he saw a man who looked down and out, he said, "Where's Ginger Brown living these days?"

"Damned if I know. She was too rich for my blood. But for a dollar, I'll tell you where to find Rosie. She'd know if anyone would."

Ki dug a dollar out of his pants and handed it to the man

who smiled, tipped his battered hat, and said, "Sorry."

Ki used a sweep kick to drop the man heavily in the dirt. When the fellow tried to rise, Ki banged him with another kick alongside the head. Banged him just hard enough to let the man know that he had entered an agreement, and it was his turn to deliver.

"Where is she?" Ki said.

"She's in the cemetery," the man said, dredging up a loose smile.

When Ki took a menacing step forward, the man raised his hands to shield his head and squealed, "But there's a new Rosie that bought the place! Only, her name used to be Martha but now she's Rosie. She was Ginger's boss. I swear it!"

Ki got his directions in a hurry and wasted no time in finding the busy brothel. It was not in the best part of town. In fact, it was in the worst part of town, where there were several mean-looking saloons and a few diseased-looking women standing beside the alleys soliciting money, favors, or both.

"Say there, big Chinese boy," a sunken-cheeked redhead cooed. "Why don't you come on into my crib and let me stroke that long black hair of yours. I could stroke something else with the tip of my tongue, for two American dollars."

Another woman laughed coarsely as the samurai hurried on past them. He entered Rosie's Place and stopped for a moment to let his eyes adjust to the poor light before he moved deeper into the smoke-filled room.

"You looking for a good time, mister?" a silken-voiced woman said as she slipped her arm around his waist.

"I'm looking for Martha," he said.

"Better not call her that. She took the name of this place

and she changed her own name. Gets mighty upset if you forget."

"Fine," Ki said. "Then I want to see the new Rosie."

The woman's cheap perfume was strong enough to ward off mosquitoes, and she was young, much too young to already have the hard, jaded expression that women in her profession wore after a few years. Her skin should have been clear and smooth, but it was lax and pancaked with makeup. Her eyes were bloodshot, her breath was foul, and her mouth had a looseness that Ki found sad.

"Mister," she said, "I'm more of a woman than Rosie and ten years friskier. So if you got the money, why don't I show you my snake dance? You provide the big snake."

She coughed a laugh at her own lewd sense of humor, but Ki just shook his head.

"I'm sorry," he said. "It's a matter that only Rosie can help me with."

"There ain't nothing she can do for a man that I haven't learned," the girl said, reaching down and running her fingers over his crotch.

She had nothing if not persistence. "You understand me? I think you're kind of cute."

Ki pushed past the woman, and she cursed under her breath. There was a bar at the rear of the room. The smoke was so thick it hung like low clouds about three feet below the ceiling, and Ki saw at least six women all scantily dressed and drinking what was probably colored water as they pretended to enjoy themselves.

One huge blond floozy tried to block Ki's path. The room was close and the air was stale and dead. The floozy must have weighed about 250 pounds, and Ki easily dodged her outstretched arms. When he reached the bar, he said, "I'm looking for Ginger Brown. Can you help me?"

"Nope. She don't work here anymore."

"All right, then point Rosie out to me."

"What do you want her for?" the bartender demanded.

He was a smart-alecky man in his early thirties, foppish-looking with a goatee and a silver front tooth. Ki disliked him at first glance. "Point her out to me before I break your fingers," he said quietly.

The bartender reared back as if he were greatly insulted. But he didn't give any indication he wanted to fight, and the best he could do was to bluster. "Mister, you can't talk to people in here like that! I'll call someone to throw you out on your tail!"

"One more time," Ki said. "Where's Rosie?"

"Over there," the bartender hissed, pointing out a slender, dark-haired woman in a low-cut lavender dress.

Ki studied the woman for a moment. She was sitting at a table sipping something and smiling as a big man in a suit with a drummer's case sitting next to him was telling some kind of funny story. Funny enough that several of the girls were giggling.

Ki waited where he stood until the story was finished. He was grateful to see Rosie get up and start toward the bar. Ki intercepted her and said, "I need to find Ginger Brown."

Up close the women looked ten years older than she had from across the room. "Sorry, buster. Ginger don't work here anymore. But I've got plenty of girls that can take you to geisha-land if that's where you want to go."

"It isn't," Ki said. "I need to find her so that she can testify that what Mando Santiago said in court was the truth."

Rosie's eyes widened and she laughed, only it wasn't funny. "Mister, you can get the hell outa my place before I put out a call for the marshal to put you in jail. I wasn't allowed into that courtroom—women of my kind don't go out in public to respectable places like that—but I got my eyes and ears open. I heard what you and that Texas beauty said. I want no part of whatever craziness possesses you to cross Jake Hammer. None at all."

"What about Ginger?" Ki asked softly. "If someone doesn't take an interest in her, she'll drown in trouble."

"She's already up to her neck in trouble," the woman said. "If she isn't dead."

Ki struggled to find some kind of words that would make this hard woman understand that she must cooperate and help him. "If nobody helps her, then it could be you next time," he said.

Rosie number two shook her head. "Don't you see how it is in Alpine, mister? It's a one-man show. There are rules, and you either play by them, or the Hammer comes down and crushes your skull."

"Then you won't help?"

"I couldn't even if I wanted to," the woman said. "I got a pretty good business here. I make pretty good money, and I don't have to go down for no man unless I want to."

"Except for Jake Hammer or Buck Timberman or maybe the judge now and then."

Rosie's pencil-thin eyebrows raised, and she snapped, "How'd you know that?"

"Just a guess." Ki shrugged. "Men who abuse power like to use power. They like to hurt people to remind them they can be hurt. When is the last time either Hammer or one of his lieutenants hurt you, Rosie?"

She just stared at him for a long moment and then she said, "Get out of my place, stranger. You're big trouble. I don't want any part of you."

Ki turned and left because there was nothing more that he could do. Outside, he paused by the door and looked back into the room. Rosie hadn't said a word, but Ki had the feeling that she knew where Ginger was and that she'd be thinking about his words and maybe about her own future.

Ki turned and left. He'd pay Rosie another visit this time tomorrow and see if she'd changed her mind. Until then, he guessed he'd just have to start asking everyone he met. Someone was bound to make a slip of the tongue or maybe try and put him out of commission if he started getting too close to the answer. It had to happen sooner or later.

Ki just hoped that it was sooner. He didn't like this town very much. There was the stench of decay here. Moral and legal decay. And the stench was originating from the source of all the power—Jake Hammer.

Ki turned in the direction that would take him to the east end of town, where a huge two-storied mansion overlooked the rest of Alpine. Without needing to ask, he was dead certain that Jake Hammer owned the mansion, even though he had a big cattle ranch. Hammer was not the sort to bury himself on the range and take a real interest in the livestock business.

No, sir! Cows and horses were not the things that would absorb a man like Jake Hammer. You could see at a glance that he was more interested in power and the manipulation of people. Of making money and controlling everything that took place along this part of the Mogollon Rim country.

To do that, you needed to be around the county seat, where you could be close enough to monitor things on a day-to-day basis.

Ki looked ahead toward the mansion. He wondered if Hammer would be in just now, and he wondered if Ginger Brown was buried on the grounds, or maybe being held hostage in one of the many rooms.

After Rosie's Place the mansion seemed like the best place to start looking for answers.

Ki stopped in the street and scratched his jaw. He saw a man with a rifle guarding the front gate, which was at least eight feet high and made out of wrought iron just like the fence surrounding the place.

Maybe it would be best to put on his ninja costume and pay a night visit to the mansion. Yes, the samurai decided, reversing his direction, that would be the best way to find out the truth. There was no sense in killing a guard when he could get inside without being seen.

No sense at all.

Chapter 7

Ki emerged from the darkness in his black ninja costume. He wore the traditional hood, and the only flesh showing was the skin around his eyes. His movement across the street was no more than a shadow, and when he reached the fence, he unwrapped his *surushin* from around his waist. The *surushin* was a six-foot length of rope with leather-covered balls attached to either end. It was a weapon that Ki used to bring down a running opponent, or when, as a ninja, a silent kill or capture was essential.

The mansion was occupied. Ki could see the silhouettes of moving figures through the drawn curtains. There had been a change of guards, two men replacing the one, and an added element of danger had presented itself when Ki had seen a pair of huge and ferocious-looking dogs coursing over the grounds.

The samurai had not seen Jake Hammer, but he was certain the man was inside. The sheriff and the judge had each paid an earlier visit and Ki would have given anything to have heard their conversation.

Ki studied the tall wrought-iron fence with its spiked top

for several moments. Atop each ten-foot post rested a small, spiked object, and the samurai decided that this was his target. He began to slowly whirl the *surushin* overhead and then hurled it upward. His throw was perfect, and one of the leather balls wrapped around the post top while the other dangled just above Ki's outstretched fingers.

Ki jumped up, grabbed the leather ball, and pulled his weight up the fence. For a moment he hung balanced on the top, then he quickly unwrapped his *surushin* and dropped silently into the guarded mansion compound.

It was about twenty yards to the mansion, and it was all open ground. Ki saw one of the dogs moving across the yard, and he froze, feeling his heart quicken. It was not that he feared the animal so much as it was that, if it saw him and began to bark, the second dog would also join the chase and he would be forced to escape because his presence would be well announced to those inside.

The dog was angling in his direction but had not yet spotted him when one of the guards at the gate whistled. The dog obediently turned and trotted over to the guard, who patted its head, then scratched behind its ear. Ki was pleased to see the animal drop to rest beside the man, and it looked as if it was content to remain in one place for a while. He would have felt much better, however, if the second dog was also where he could keep an eye on it.

Ki made a final inspection of his weapons. Besides the star blades and the *surushin*, which he now rewrapped around his waist, he was armed with his knife and one of his favorite fighting weapons, the *nunchaku*. *Nunchaku* were a pair of flat, heavy sticks that fit perfectly together and were connected by a few inches of braided horsehair. The advantages of the *nunchaku* were that they were very easy to conceal, and when one stick whirled as the other was held, it became a lethal weapon. In close fighting, the *nunchaku* could also be used to thrust into a man's face or catch his hands or other bones and crunch them like a nutcracker.

Satisfied that his weapons were in order, Ki studied a drainpipe attached to the outside wall, just a few feet north of the fireplace. The samurai took another look around for the second dog, then decided that he could wait no longer. Unsheathing his *tanto* knife, he moved soundlessly across the yard, his eyes fixed to the drainpipe that would carry him up past a second-story window that was partially opened.

The samurai was almost at the mansion when he heard an ominous rumble, and then, as he jumped for the drainpipe, he felt the bite of powerful jaws on his lower leg.

His ninja costume was ripped and he winced in pain, but made no sound as the fangs of the beast sank deep into the muscles of his calf. Ki released the drainpipe and landed on one leg. The dog was so powerful that it wrenched him to the earth, and then it released its bite and lunged for his throat. Ki blocked the animal with his left forearm, and his right hand swept up and buried the knife into the ferocious beast's throat.

A torrent of warm blood coursed down on him, but the animal's jaws locked on his forearm, and Ki had to slice the jugular vein and then the beast's thick jaw muscles until its body went limp and it released it's hold.

He pushed the dog aside, angry that he had not been able to disable the animal with his *nunchaku* sticks, but knowing that there simply had not been time. His leg throbbed and he knew that it as well as his forearm were bleeding copiously and that he was now disabled and could not move or fight as well as he should. Pushing the pain and his own disappointment out of his mind, he jumped upward, grabbed the drainpipe and hauled himself silently up to the second-story open window.

He grabbed the windowsill and dangled for a moment before he managed to push the window up high enough to allow him entry. Ki had not seen any shadows crossing behind this window, and he sure hoped that the room was unoccupied as he pulled himself inside, then toppled onto a Persian rug.

There was a lamp flickering in the room, and it's light confirmed what he already knew—he was a mess. His forearm was bleeding enough to cause blood to run down to his hand and make gripping objects far more difficult. His damaged leg was not responding quite properly, and his ninja costume was soaked and ripped by the beast's sharp fangs.

Ki looked around the room and saw a porcelain pitcher and a wash basin. He struggled to his feet and moved over to it, then poured cool water into the basin and washed blood from his nasty wounds. Using his *tanto* blade, he cut strips from the black ninja costume and hurriedly bound his injuries, then dried himself completely.

He could hear the sound of voices downstairs, and when he took a better look around the room, he realized that whoever was using it could reappear at any moment. Ki ignored the impulse to move with haste. Instead, he paused and gathered his wits and made himself calm inside. He reminded himself again that he was ninja. That he had been taught by Hirata, the great one who had taken pity on a small, ostracized boy to save his life and teach him the true samurai's ways.

Hirata had been a mountain of muscle, a mountain of strength. Once a proud samurai, when he had found Ki, he had been the lowest of all men—a *ronin*, which meant a "wave man." A *ronin* was a samurai without a noble master to serve and protect. *Ronin* were as meaningless and purposeless as the tossing waves on the surface of a vast, storm ocean. *Ronin* owned nothing. They were nothing. They belonged to nothing.

But Hirata had possessed an unwavering dignity. And through the outcast, half-white, half-Japanese boy, Hirata had renewed himself with some small purpose, and by the time that he committed *seppuku*, "suicide by ritual disembowelment," he had lovingly created a new samurai from the ravages of a starving boy.

Ki gathered himself and seemed to lift a little taller. Hirata had always taught him that adversity was the milk, the bread, and even the honey of life. Adversity was the thing that made it worth living. Without adversity, usually unexpected, a man grew lax in mind and body. It was the nature of the universe that all living things should be tested continuously. Those that did not meet the test perished, those that fought and claimed victory, claimed it only so that they might live another day and be tested all over again, and again, until, inevitably, they failed in either body or spirit.

Hirata had believed that and so did Ki.

Well, the samurai thought, this is adversity. Nothing yet has gone quite as I expected, but I will survive and I will emerge victorious. It is not my karma to die like a sneak-thief in this corrupt town.

Ki moved to the door and slowly pulled it open. He could distinguish individual voices now, and he recognized one of them as belonging to Jake Hammer. Ki dropped down in a crouch and moved forward to peer over the second-story landing, where he saw a gathering of what were obviously very prosperous ranchers.

It appeared that Jake Hammer was holding court with his minions, because his voice was louder and more authoritative than the others. "What we need to do," he said, "is simply to take out the Mexican families one by one. Quietly, without any fuss or publicity, we just wipe them off the face of the earth. We eradicate them like vermin."

"What about the women and the children?" someone asked.

"Vermin are vermin," Hammer said quietly. "If some of them want to jump ship and return to Old Mexico, we won't stop them. But if they insist on staying, they'll just have to face the consequences."

"I don't hold much with killing kids!"

"Little Mexicans grow up to be big Mexicans," Hammer snapped. "And they'll keep giving us trouble until they're all gone. We offered to buy them all out, but they wouldn't listen. They had their chance."

There was a general rumble of agreement except for one man who protested, "Getting rid of them ain't all that easy. Word of trouble gets out, even off the Mogollon Rim. Hell, that Starbuck woman that Buck's got in his jail could sound the alarm and bring us big trouble. Sure a good thing that the telegraph operator saw fit not to send that message to the governor of Texas asking for help."

Ki swore silently. He should have known that the man would type some nonsense into the lines and trick him into thinking his message had gotten out of Alpine. Well, at least he knew that there wasn't any help coming from outside. They would have to depend upon themselves, which was the way the samurai liked it anyhow.

"I don't want anyone to worry about Miss Starbuck," Hammer said, puffing on a long cigar. "I mean to handle her personally."

Several of the ranchers laughed.

"We'll just bet you will. Wouldn't mind 'taking care of her' myself for a few nights."

More laughter and then Hammer said, "Gentlemen, when we take out the Mexicans, we'll be dividing up more rangle and timberland than we now own all together. We know that the Spanish land grants are a farce. They were given out by a foreign power to men who courted favor and often just plain kissed some Spanish official's fat ass. We're Americans and this is American territory. The Supreme Court hasn't seen fit to strip those Mexicans of their land holdings, but we know that's wrong and we're going to make it right."

The cattlemen nodded in agreement, but one said, "Sure wish we could do it without any more bloodshed. Shootin', then ropin' and dragging Juan Santiago to death goes against my grain. And we lost two men over it!"

"It was the samurai," Hammer said. "I've read about him, and he's a dangerous man. That's why I've got a couple of guards and dogs outside."

"Well, what are you going to do about him?"

"I'm not going to do anything," Hammer said. "Not until tomorrow when I spring Miss Starbuck out of jail and then offer her and her samurai friend a one-way ticket out of Alpine. If she takes it, and she will if she's as smart as she's supposed to be, then the samurai can go along with her, and we'll wash our hands of the matter."

"You mean you intend to just let the samurai go after he killed two of our men! Why hellfire, Jake! What are the other gunnies going to think?"

Hammer's voice took on a hard edge. "They'll think they'd better be more careful in their work. They get paid top fighting wages to take chances. Even the Mexicans will kill a few before this fight is all over."

The one who'd objected lapsed into brooding silence for a moment, then said, "What about Ben Rodgers? That big sonofabitch is like a bullet in a campfire. You never know

70

when he's going to explode. Even worse, the Mexicans are starting to look up to him even though he ain't one of them."

Hammer scowled. "I'm going to send Buck Timberman and a few of his deputies up into the mountains. They've got hunting dogs that will sniff him out, and they can tree him like a mountain cat and drop him like a hot iron."

"It won't be easy. Not even for Buck," another rancher said. "That big sonofabitch can shoot the eye out of a tree squirrel at a hundred yards."

"There are ways to skin every cat," Hammer said, sipping on a glass of amber liquor. "For example, we all know that Rodgers has a soft spot for animals. So all Buck and his boys have to do is just shoot a few of his sheep and keep shooting them until Rodgers comes running out."

The other ranchers exchanged somber glances. Being the owners of livestock, maybe they did not cotton to the idea of shooting another man's animals, even if they were nothing but sheep. But no one posed an objection to the plan, and then the conversation lapsed into the poor cattle prices and the prospects of getting a few summer rains, which would sure help the feed situation.

Ki did not listen to any more talk. One by one he began a hurried search of each room. He had a feeling that, if Ginger was still alive, she'd be locked in some upstairs bedroom, probably until they decided what to do with her. Killing sheep was one thing, but killing an innocent woman—even a pretty prostitute—was something else again, and Ki figured that they might be stalling.

There were six upstairs bedrooms, and damned if Ki didn't have to go to them all before he tried the last door and found it locked. He turned the knob as hard as he could, but it was made well and it would not yield or break.

Ki was trying to decide if he should pull out his knife and try to jimmy the lock when he heard the creak of steps on the stairs. He jumped back, found the closest door, and barely managed to slip inside when someone reached the upstairs landing.

Ki stood behind the door and waited silently for someone to enter. But no one did, and then he heard a woman's cry of pain and the sound of flesh striking flesh through the wall.

The samurai moved over to the wall adjoining this room with the one that was locked. He listened; it wasn't hard to overhear a conversation, because the walls were thin.

"What the hell were you doing against the door!" Hammer demanded.

"I . . . I heard the doorknob turn. I thought it was you and that maybe you'd lost the key. I was going to open the door when you burst inside."

Another slapping sound and cry. The samurai stiffened as Hammer shouted, "Damn liar! You were trying to escape. You can't get out of the window without killing yourself in a fall, so you were thinking about sneaking out on the landing and trying to escape."

"No, I wasn't, Jake! I swear it. I know you've got dogs and men posted outside. I couldn't get away even if I tried."

Hammer's voice softened. "I'm glad to hear you say that, because it's true."

"So what are you going to do with me?"

"Nothing until Mando Santiago is sent to prison. After that, you can go back to Rosie's Place and keep working."

"I'd rather move on," she said. "I . . . I just need a change of scenery."

"Don't act stupid," Hammer snarled. "If we let you go, you could tell anybody what really happened and maybe

72

get Mando set free. No, sir, you can either stay here and keep working at your trade, or I'll find a way to make sure you can't ever talk."

There was a long silence and then the woman said, "I'll stay. I'll stay here until I'm old and used up, Mr. Hammer. I swear I won't say anything about what happened. Mando wasn't anything to me. Really he wasn't."

"I'm not too sure about that," Hammer said. "But why don't you get in bed and try to convince me you're telling the truth."

The bed must have been pushed right up against the wall because Ki heard the springs creaking faster and faster.

"Mr. Hammer, why don't I just stay here? I don't need to go back to Rosie's."

The bedsprings stopped creaking for a moment, and then Ki heard the cattleman laugh. "Now, why should I keep you here?"

"For this!" she said.

"Hell, Ginger, you're not going to stay pretty much longer. Then I'd have me a used-up whore that I didn't want. No deal."

"Bastard!" she cried.

Hammer must have done something cruel because Ginger shrieked with pain and then began to sob.

"You're just a whore, Ginger. So quit thinking about being something decent. Just shut up and do what you do best!"

Ginger didn't say another word, but Hammer did. He started groaning louder and louder until he finally shouted, "Oh, yeah!"

After that it was quiet until Ki heard footsteps, and several minutes later the door opened and closed. Ki rushed to his own door, prepared to jump Hammer if the man came into this room. But Hammer had another bedroom and walked past.

Ki knew that he could not afford to wait any longer. There was a dead dog down beside the house, and its body was going to be discovered by its companion pretty soon. In fact, it was surprising that it had not already been discovered. Time was wasting. What Ki had to do was to get Ginger Brown out of this house, across the yard, and over the fence or through the front gate.

The samurai wasn't at all sure that he could get himself out of this place, let alone the woman. But he was going to try, and if he failed, it was going to be the end.

Chapter 8

Ki slipped back out into the hallway, and this time Ginger Brown's locked door was less of a problem because when the samurai knocked softly, the woman came to the door and unlocked it. "Jake, what . . ."

She opened her mouth to cry out, but Ki clamped his hand across her lips and pushed her back into the room so hard she tripped and fell. Before she could recover, he closed the door and jumped on her, again clamping his hand over her mouth.

She struggled, but he had her pinned to the floor. The young woman was strong, slick with the perspiration of lovemaking, and frightened bad enough to give the samurai quite a tussle.

"Stop it!" he hissed. "I'm not interested in raping you, woman! I come to help."

She stilled and her eyes glared suspiciously up at him.

"I'm your only chance of getting out of Alpine alive. You know that, sooner or later, Jake Hammer will have you murdered. Given that reality, can I trust you to be silent if I take my hand from your mouth?"

He raised the palm of his right hand from her mouth just a fraction of an inch, and she blurted angrily, "Who or what the fuck are you!"

"I'm a samurai," he said, unperturbed by her coarseness.

"You're a mess and covered with . . . ugh! Blood!"

He tightened his hand down on her mouth and buried a scream. "Listen, you fool!" he said in a harsh undertone. "Some of the blood belongs to one of Hammer's vicious guard dogs. The rest of it is mine from where he bit me while I was trying to save you."

He shifted his weight on her. She was soft and had a beautiful figure; Ki had to admit that, even under these desperate circumstances, she was highly desirable. Her breasts were large and the nipples were as firm and prominent as blueberries. She had a raw, almost animalistic magnetism, and her eyes were a glittering blue, her hair a light brown. There were bruises on her face and her full lips were puffy from the blows she had just taken from Jake Hammer, but a man scarcely noticed because of her obvious physical attributes.

Ki reluctantly rolled off of her. She wasn't going to scream now. Her angry expression had changed into one of confusion. She remained on the floor exactly as she had fallen while Ki knelt before her on his knees. "I haven't got time to explain everything, and even if I did you wouldn't believe it."

"Wait!" she exclaimed softly. "You are the samurai!"

Ki blinked. "That's right, but—"

"The cattlemen have been talking about you all day," she said. "And I heard the guards out by the gate talking about you to each other. They say you killed two men up at Butte Station."

"I tried to save Juan Santiago," Ki admitted. "I failed."

She sat up slowly, crossing first her shapely legs and then her arms across her big breasts. "And now you want to try and save me. What are you, some sort of Oriental Don Quixote?"

He almost allowed himself a smile. "No, and since I barely made it up a drainpipe tonight, I doubt I'd do any better tilting at windmills. What I am doesn't matter. What does matter is that you are a dead man, and Mando Santiago might as well be dead if you don't testify in his behalf."

"Oh, no," she said, scooting away from him and shaking her head. "I'd rather be an Alpine, Arizona, whore than a corpse. So thanks for your offer to help, but no, thanks."

Ki frowned. "I was hoping you'd be cooperative."

"You must have been hoping I was brain-damaged if you think I'd go along with some crazy attempt to get me out of here alive. There is still at least one man-eating dog down there, mister. And there's also a roomful of cattlemen, every one of which was practically born on a horse with a gun in his fist." Ginger shook her head emphatically. "Uh-uh, mister. I'm staying put."

"Sorry to hear that," Ki said, coming to his feet. "Here, let me at least help you up."

He offered her his hand, which she took, and then, before she quite realized it, he reached out and dug his thumb into a soft place at the base of her lovely neck. Her blue eyes fluttered and she sagged back to the floor.

Ki found her a dress and wasted several precious but interesting minutes trying to pull it on over her head. It was hard work trying to dress a beautiful but unconscious woman. It was much more fun undressing them when they were wide awake.

He propped her up against the wall and dug his shoulder

into her nice little tummy, then he stood up, hobbling badly on his strong leg and testing the bitten one to see if it was going to betray him after a few steps.

Ki was simply not sure what he was going to do next. It would be impossible to go out the landing and down the stairs, because the cattlemen were right down below. A healthy and unencumbered ninja could have slipped past them in the blink of an eye, but not a ninja carrying a hundred pounds of woman on one good leg and one that was badly chewed.

The samurai hobbled over to the window. There was no drainpipe nearby to cling to, but there was a narrow ledge that skirted around a corner and disappeared. To what? A dead end or some avenue of escape?

There was only one way to find out, so Ki dumped Ginger on the bed, removed his soft ninja sandals, and slipped outside. The ledge was only about eighteen inches wide, and it would be a bad fall to the yard below if he took a misstep. But he did not, and when he came to the corner, he found it easier to edge around than he'd expected, and he was rewarded for his efforts to see that it met a sloping part of the roofline.

The samurai hurried back into the room, picked up the girl, threw her over his shoulder, and managed to get outside. Now things suddenly became much trickier. Her body had to be positioned and balanced just perfectly so that it did not pull him out into the air, nor drag along the wall and bump him off the narrow ledge.

Ki felt sweat pour from his body. He felt weak, and he dared not look down. He was sure that, if he fell, he could land properly and break his fall, but the unconscious young woman he carried would be killed on impact.

His bare feet slid along the ledge, groping like so many little fingers. Fortunately, his wounds had stopped bleeding, so at least the ledge was not slippery with his blood. He kept his eyes straight ahead and concentrated on feel and touch rather than sight. His body was in perfect condition except for the leg and the wounded arm, and he slowly negotiated his way along the ledge until he came to the corner, and that was where he stopped.

Taking a deep breath, he tried to slip around the corner, but either the woman's head or her feet kept hanging him up. Ki struggled and struggled, almost losing his balance several times.

After five agonizing minutes, he knew that he could not round the corner with the woman draped over his shoulder. He would either have to return or set her down and try to carry her around the corner upright, or else he would have to wait until she regained consciousness and then see if she could help herself to the rooftop just a few feet beyond the sharp bend.

Ki spent five heart-pounding minutes getting the woman off his shoulder and onto her feet. He leaned her against the wall and pinned her there with his own weight. He had not realized it, but his chest was heaving with exertion and he was wringing wet. He forced himself to look down into the yard. In the shadows about fifty feet to the north, he fancied he could see the dark outline of the dog he had been forced to kill.

Where was the second guard dog? Still at the gate keeping the guard company? And if it was, how long could he expect that to last?

"Ginger," he said, whispering loudly into her ear. "Wake up now."

The woman did not respond. Ki swore with helplessness. Hirata had taught him how to quickly find all the human pressure points so that he could render a man or woman unconscious almost instantly, as he had just done.

But undoing the damage was a subject that Hirata had not covered.

He tried pinching her flesh and that got an immediate response. After three hard pinches, Ginger snapped awake and clawed at his face.

Ki pinned her against the wall. "Look down, dammit!"

She froze. Looked out at the open air and then at the stars, and finally down to the yard below. "Oh, my Lord!" she whispered. "Get me off of here!"

"To your left, around the corner," he said, forcing her ahead of him.

"But . . ."

He nudged her hard enough that she cried out in panic, but she did edge around the corner, and then she saw the sloping roofline and quickly scurried to safety.

"Are you mad!" she whispered. "What . . ."

She didn't finish, because the howl of the remaining guard dog filled the air.

"They'll be coming along any minute," Ki said. "And when they find that dead guard dog, the alarm will sound, and it will be ten times harder to get out of here."

"I'm going back to my room!"

"No, you're not! You're getting out of here with me. You've everything to gain now and absolutely nothing to lose. Hammer will figure you had to cooperate to get around that corner, and he'll kill you for sure. All they've been waiting for is one good excuse."

Ginger swallowed and her eyes grew round with fear. "You're right," she said in a voice dull with defeat. "We're as good as dogmeat already."

"No, we're not," Ki said. "We're going to take advantage of the confusion and make a dash for the gate."

"From up here!"

"Of course not!" he snapped, grabbing her hand and

leading her quickly across the steeply sloped roof.

Ki found a place where they could jump down to the porch roof, and he wasted no time in getting Ginger to come along. However, they landed harder than he'd expected, and the samurai's bad leg folded under him, and he rolled off the roof and dropped ten feet to crash into some bushes. Ginger must have thought that he had planned it that way, because she came right behind.

As they clawed their way out of the bushes, they could hear men shouting and the surviving guard dog barking crazily. Ki knew that they had no more than a few seconds to make good their escape. He grabbed Ginger's hand and hobbled madly around the corner to run right into someone who started to shout.

Ki was unable to deliver a foot strike, so he lunged forward, pulling the *nunchaku* out of his tunic. The free end of the weapon whirred ominously, but was abruptly silenced as it cracked against the startled man's head, dropping him to the earth.

"Did you kill him!" Ginger cried. "Oh, no! They'll—"

"Come on!" Ki shouted, racing for the gate on one leg. As he had hoped, the excited guard had followed his dog around the house and left the front gate unmanned. The exit onto the main street of Alpine was theirs for the taking.

They were twenty feet from the gate when the second guard dog came skidding around the house running low and hard, his teeth bared and fire in his eyes. The samurai sensed the dog, and he whirled and yelled, "Keep running for the gate! Don't stop!"

The dog did not even slow as it launched itself directly for Ki's throat. Once again the *nunchaku* whirred ominously, and then its voice was silenced by impact. The dog's momentum carried him into Ki at chest level and knocked him down. Ki bounced back on one leg and followed Ginger out through the gate and down the street.

"Find us a hiding place!" he shouted. "This is *your* town, not mine!"

"It's Jake Hammer's town. There's no where to run!"

"Then grab that horse and let's ride!"

The saddled horse was tied before a house. The young cowboy that owned the horse was sitting on the porch steps with a young lady. When Ginger reached the animal and started to untie the reins, the man shouted, "Hey! Stop that!"

But Ginger didn't listen. She tore the reins free and tossed them over the animal's head and neck, then jammed her foot in the stirrup.

The cowboy vaulted the porch railing, and Ki went for him. Their bodies crashed together, and they broke through a picket fence. The woman on the porch screamed, and her shrill, frightened voice seemed to pierce the night all over Alpine.

Ki had all he could handle with the young man. They rolled over twice, and Ki groaned because he felt the thorns of a rose garden rip his flesh and tear his ninja outfit even more than it was already torn. The cowboy was wiry and strong, and he butted Ki in the face, trying to break his nose.

The samurai found himself on the bottom, and he punched up with stiff fingers aiming for the softness of the man's throat. But his opponent was a seasoned fighter. The cowboy dipped his chin and deflected what should have been a decisive blow. He sledged downward with his fist and caught the samurai on the side of the head.

For a moment Ki lost consciousness, and then he heard Ginger's cry of anger as she jumped from the saddle and landed on the cowboy's back and tried to rake his eyes out.

"Let go of him!" she screamed. "Get off of him!"

Ki took advantage of the distraction and kicked his good leg up, hooking the bigger man under the chin with his heel. He dragged the cowboy over backward, then jumped on him and delivered a chop to the base of the man's neck.

His opponent shook his head in a daze, and Ki's right hand slashed down again, and this time the cowboy went down for the rest of the night.

"Did you kill him, too?" Ginger cried.

"No," the samurai panted, "but Hammer and his men are going to kill us in about fifteen seconds if we don't get out of town."

As if to emphasize his warning, gunfire punctuated the night air. The woman on the porch kept screaming as Ginger somehow crawled back on the skitterish horse and pulled Ki up behind her before sending the animal racing into the darkness with bullets probing their wake.

"We made it!" Ginger cried as the lights of Alpine faded behind them. "We actually made it!"

"So far we have," Ki said, holding on behind the woman and letting her rein the stampeding horse. "Now all we have to do is find a place to run and hide."

Chapter 9

They rode through the heavy forest for what seemed like hours, and when Ki could hear their horse starting to labor badly, he ordered Ginger to rein it down to a walk.

"There's a lot of mesas in this wild country anyway," he said. "It's no place to be galloping a horse in the dark."

Ginger sighed. "I must have been insane to come out here like this. They'll find us. Jake has at least one man on his payroll that can track pretty good. At first light he will lead the others up our backtrail and we'll be buzzard-bait before midafternoon."

"Are you always so cheerful?" Ki asked dryly.

"No," she admitted, "but then, I've never been in this much trouble before. I should have stayed with Jake and taken my chances. . . ."

"You had no chance with that man. He'd have killed you eventually. Ginger, you did the right thing," Ki said, wanting to encourage her.

"It's done," she said. "There's no turning back now. I just wish I hadn't gotten involved in the whole mess. I was saving all my money. I was going to go away and get respectability."

Ginger shook her head. "That's every whore's dream, isn't it? To run away and become clean and new again. To be reborn and to fall in love and marry a good man."

"I suppose it is," Ki said quietly. "It's not impossible. And as for your money, is it in the bank?"

"Yes."

"Then it'll still be there when this is over."

"Not very damn likely," she said. "Jake Hammer is the principal owner of the only bank in town. He'll take everything I saved."

"Then I'll get it back for you," Ki promised.

"I'll say one thing," Ginger offered, "you aren't short on confidence. But then, Mando wasn't, either, and look where it got him."

"The game has yet to be played out," Ki told her. "We just lost on the first deal. We've got plenty of time to win."

"Like hell we do. We'll most likely be dead by this time tomorrow."

Ki knew there was no sense in arguing the point. The way things were right now, odds were that they would soon be dead.

Wanting to change the subject, he said, "How did you get involved with Mando? I had the feeling that Mexicans would be strung up by the testicles if one ever tried to visit a white woman."

"I don't know. Mando just caught my eye. Before the bad trouble began, he used to come around with Juan, and they'd ask Rosie if they could do odd jobs. They were my age, but seemed like innocent boys back then. They were polite and didn't act like they were better than me. As for Mando himself, there was just something about him that attracted me. Unlike any of the rest of them, he had a certain . . . I don't know."

"Dignity?"

"Yeah, but I'd say he also had flair and as much self-confidence as I've ever seen in any man. One time he admitted that he considered himself to be equal to anyone, but no better than anyone. He talked to a whore like me the same way he'd talk to a lady. And he treated the town drunk with the same respect that he treated Jake Hammer. The color of a man's skin meant nothing to him."

Ki nodded. "I know something about how it feels to have men judge you by the color of your skin, or the shape of your nose or eyes. It can hurt if you don't believe in yourself."

"You do and so does Mando," Ginger said. "You even remind me a lot of him. The way you move. The way you both act. Mando would have come after me if he hadn't been locked in jail."

Ginger was silent for a moment, and then she blurted, "They'll kill him, you know."

"He's been sentenced to life in the Yuma Prison."

"He'll never reach it," she said in a voice that was chillingly confident.

"Why?"

"He just won't," she said. "They'll stage an escape attempt from the stage he rides and gun him down somewhere between here and Yuma. I know how Jake Hammer thinks and acts. I know that smooth sonofabitch all too well."

Her voice was sad, and Ki had an impulse to touch her bruised cheek, so he did.

"Hey! What did you do that for?"

"I just felt like it," he said.

"Well, I'm not of a mind to spend my last few hours

doing for free what I've always had to do for a living, if you know what I mean."

"I know what you mean," Ki said. "And that wasn't what I had in mind. I was thinking about how you jumped off this horse and landed on that cowboy's back. I don't usually need help, but I was in some trouble."

"Damn right you were," she said. "That particular cowboy was Rowdy Hoag. He's one of the toughest men on the whole damn rim. And one of the strongest, too. I've wrestled with him a time or two. And believe me, I got pinned for as long as he wanted me to be pinned."

Ki frowned. "Did you grow up here?"

"Sure. Why else would a woman stay around?"

"What happened?"

She rode along about a mile before she answered. "My father was one of them."

"Them?"

"One of Hammer's friends. Only back then it was Jake's father. Anyway, the cattlemen raided a Mexican sheep camp maybe ten years ago, and they rimrocked a flock over the edge of a mesa. Same as they do now. The sheepherder tending that flock could have run away, but he stood and tried to fight. He was gunned down."

Ginger swallowed noisily, and Ki felt her shudder as she continued: "It turned out the 'he' was a 'she' and only about sixteen years old. Nobody felt good about it—especially my father. It ate him alive."

"Did he think he had killed her?" Ki asked.

"He didn't know, and maybe that was the worst part of it," Ginger said. "He had fired a few shots at the girl, just like the others. He could have even been the one that killed her and just that possibility destroyed him."

"What happened to your mother?"

"She couldn't stand what my father was doing to

himself... all the drinking. The waking up at night in a cold sweat. She tried to take me away with her, but I couldn't leave my father. I was always his pet. I stayed with him until the bitter end, when he put a bullet through his brain."

"I'm sorry."

Ginger expelled a deep breath. "I tried to hold on to our ranch, but my cattle kept disappearing. Finally I just gave it all up and moved into town. I stayed in a boardinghouse until the money ran out. And then... well, you can guess the rest of the story."

"But you liked Mando."

"Yeah," she whispered. "He was the only decent person in Alpine, as far as I was concerned. He was a gentleman, even to me. And when he looked into my eyes, I saw things that I never saw in any other man's eyes."

Ki heard her sob, and he wrapped his arms around her and pressed his face into her hair. "You're a good woman," he said. "I know you don't believe that, but Mando does and so do I."

"Aw, go to hell," she sniffled. "And let's try and think of some way to save our lives. What for, I'm not sure. But let's at least try."

"We'll do more than try," Ki vowed. "We'll succeed. And we'll live to see the conspiracy of cattle ranchers broken and the rights of everyone restored."

"Jeezus," she whispered. "An Oriental optimist! Aren't you some piece of work, though."

Ki chuckled. If he wasn't careful, he was going to fall in love with this girl.

When dawn arrived, they stared out on a huge, broken land of canyons, mesas, jagged peaks, and forests as thick as meadow grass. They dismounted beside a sparkling mountain stream and let their weary horse drink its fill, then they hobbled the animal in a nearby meadow and let it graze for a while and try to regain its strength for what might be a hard race later in the day.

"Do you have any idea where we are?" Ginger asked, chewing on a piece of grass and staring at the mountains and the way the sunrise gilded the snow on their summits.

"We're moving northwest," Ki said. "Somewhere ahead is desert. Tucson would be southwest of us at least a couple of hundred miles. But the territorial capital at Prescott is closer."

"Is that where we're heading?"

"I guess," the samurai told her.

"You don't sound very sure of that," Ginger said with a frown. "You don't sound near as confident as you did last night."

"All right," Ki said. "I think the best thing to do is to try and reach the governor in Prescott. If you can at least plead Mando's case and set the record straight, we'll have done as much as we can for now."

"What good will that do if they set him up for an ambush?"

"I'll go back after you're safe and out of Hammer's reach," Ki said. "I'll try and stop them."

"You don't look at all well enough to stop anybody from doing anything," Ginger said with a worried look on her pretty face.

"My leg and arm pain me and I feel hot," he admitted.

Ginger reached out and touched his forehead. "You're feverish. Let me see that leg."

Ki rolled up his pants leg. The dog bite was not pretty. The beast had ripped his fangs deep into muscle.

"It's infected," Ginger said. "It looks real bad. Let me see your arm."

He rolled up his sleeve. The arm was also badly swollen and discolored.

"We need to find you a doctor," she said. "And we need to do it fast."

Ki shook his head. "I'm afraid this country out here is a little short of doctors."

"I'll try and clean it up as best I can," Ginger said, not sounding very optimistic. "But those bites need more than a little cleaning. You need some medicine."

Ki didn't argue with her. He laid back on the grass while she tore a couple of strips from her dress and tried to wash both the wounds. It didn't hurt at all. He closed his eyes and stared up at a cloudless sky and tried to think about how he could get out of this mess.

"Maybe we should double back to Alpine," he said. "They wouldn't expect that."

"Dumb idea," she snapped.

"You got a better one?"

"We look for help," she said. "And the only ones that will help us are the sheepmen. If I see a flock or a sign of their passing, I think we should try and reach their camp."

"Why?" Ki asked. "They're not doctors, and we'd only bring them our own trouble."

"Maybe they'd have some medicine," she said hopefully. "Or know how to make some."

"You're reaching for straws," Ki told her. "The main thing is that you get away and reach the territorial capital in Prescott."

"We won't make it," Ginger said. "Not before you either pass out with a fever or this horse of ours quits or goes lame. Did you notice that he's already thrown a shoe in this rocky country?"

"I noticed," Ki said.

"It doesn't matter," Ginger told him. "We'll be overtaken anyway."

Ki closed his eyes. The woman was probably right, but there was no point in dwelling on the fact. "I'm going to take a short nap," he said. "Don't let me sleep more than an hour. The horse needs that long to graze."

"Go ahead and sleep," she told him as she rinsed a rag in the cool stream and came back to place it on his forehead. "It will do you good."

Ki reached out and touched her arm. "Take heart," he said. "I've been in a whole lot worse situations than this and come out alive."

"Well, I haven't," she said. "But I'll try and keep up my spirits. Do you have a weapon in case someone comes along?"

Ki's hand slipped into his tunic, stiff with dried blood. He pulled out a star blade and gave it to her.

"What's this for?"

"It's a weapon," he told her.

"It might as well be a Mexican spur rowel for all the good it would do for me against Jake's boys."

Ki returned the star blade to the inside pocket of his tunic. He really saw no point at all in showing her the *nunchaku* or the *surushin* wrapped around his waist.

Chapter 10

When Ginger mopped his brow again and roused the samurai into wakefulness, the sun was much higher.

"You let me sleep much more than an hour," Ki complained, feeling as if he were lying face-up on the hot desert sands with the sun baking his brains. "You shouldn't have let me sleep so long."

"You needed the sleep," she said. "You look even worse than I do."

"Help me up and let's ride," Ki told her as he pushed weakly to his feet only to discover that his infected leg was on fire and his arm was swollen up like a rotting cucumber.

Ginger brought the horse over and somehow managed to help get the samurai into the saddle. She climbed up behind the cantle and put her arms around Ki's waist, more to hold him upright than for her own support.

The horse moved out smartly and seemed much rested. They rode at a steady trot, but soon Ki was gripping the saddlehorn and trying his damnedest to keep from toppling to the ground.

"You can't go on like this," Ginger said, trying to fight

down her own panic. "Ki, you're killing yourself."

"We've got to get you to Prescott," he replied thickly.

But three miles farther on, he blacked out and tumbled over to strike the rocky ground.

"Are you all right?" Ginger cried, lifting his head to her lap.

"No," he said. "And it seems pretty obvious that you must go on alone. Head straight in the direction we were riding, and you're bound to come on a ranch or some little town. Get to Prescott!"

"But I can't just leave you!"

Ki's voice grew hard. "If you stay here, they'll just kill us both. If that happens, even Mando is going to die for certain and no one will be punished. Everything will have been for nothing."

Ginger bit her lower lip. "All right. But first I'll get the canteen that was tied on the saddle, and I'll fill it with cold water and leave it for you to drink. I'll find help as soon as I can, and when I do, I'll come back for you."

"Get to Prescott!" he said, shaking violently.

Ginger unstrapped the canteen from the saddle. It was half empty, and she wanted to leave Ki as much water as she possibly could. Just over the hill there might be another stream.

She scrambled up a ridge, and she was faint and out of breath even before she reached the top. Because of the altitude the air was very thin, but when she topped the summit, she cried out with happiness to see a flock of sheep and big Ben Rodgers with his dogs.

"Hey!" she shouted, her voice echoing up and down the valleys and over the ridges. "Hey, Ben!"

The man snatched up his rifle and dived sideways into some rabbitbrush all in one motion. A moment later, when he recognized her, he emerged as his dogs gathered protectively around his flock. It was as if they had been through this any number of times and knew exactly what to do.

Ginger ran down the hill, aware that she was only half dressed and looked a fright. The giant sheepman stood with his feet planted a yard apart and watched her come. He said something to his dogs, and they stopped barking, and instead of a growl, Ginger was greeted by the wag of their tails.

She had seen Ben before, but not since she had become a prostitute in Alpine. The last time she'd seen Ben was when she was sixteen and living on her father's cattle ranch. Ben Rodgers had been the enemy then, too, and he had always been elusive and mysterious. He had always stayed out of rifle range, as big and as wild as a rogue and cattle-killing grizzly bear.

The man was rumored to be the finest rifleman in all of the territory. Some said he had been a mountain man and a friend of Jim Bridger and John Colter. Others said no, that he had been a famous buffalo hunter for the transcontinental railroad and had grown sick of the slaughter and had become Indian for a time.

Others said he was crazy and a mad killer running from the law or maybe the Pinkertons for murders in ten different states and territories.

Ginger didn't believe any of the stories—and she believed them all. How could you fathom a legend? Now, even as she approached him, she wondered if he were anything like normal men. Had he ever been a boy? Had he ever loved a woman? Had he ever cried, sung, or laughed? Had it not been for Ki and the fact that he would die without help, she would have raced away faster than a spirit. Fled from this man as if he were the devil himself.

In her childhood, at even from a great distance, Ben Rodgers had seemed as lasting as a mountain, and as she drew near and prepared to talk with him for the first time, he still seemed like a mountain, only a much craggier one. He was dressed in the same buckskin breeches, shirt, and moccasins, and he carried the same big rifle. But unlike before, his beard and black hair were sprinkled with silver and his massive shoulders were a little humped with age and hard work. His eyebrows were mostly gray, and they matched his eyes. His mouth seemed too small, but it was not a cruel mouth. Not at all.

"You're Ben Rodgers," she said stupidly.

He neither confirmed nor denied the statement. His eyes seemed to move at and through her.

"I need your help," she said, wringing her hands together and dredging up all her courage. "There is a man on the other side of that ridge, and he is dying of a fever."

Ben turned and started to walk away.

"Please!" she called. "He's a *good* man! We're being hunted down by Jake Hammer's men. They can't be so far behind us right now."

Rodgers stopped, pivoted in his moccasins, and rumbled. "You brought the Hammer men onto my ranch?"

"We didn't know it was your ranch! Honest! We didn't see any signs posted or anything at all. We ran for our lives, Mr. Rodgers!"

She had never babbled like this to anyone before. She couldn't stop talking. "We didn't mean to bring you trouble. Honest! We were trying to get to Prescott to save Mando Santiago. But we ran out of time."

Ben frowned and considered her words for almost a full minute. Then he turned back toward his flock and whistled three times, loud and sharp as his massive upraised arm made a circling motion and then stopped, pointing to the north.

Ginger momentarily forgot her fear. In amazement she

watched the sheepdogs circle the flock and drive them north. Up a long grade, through a stand of aspen, and then, bleats receding to silence, to vanish over a mountaintop.

"They understood! They're taking the sheep out of danger."

"They're smarter than most people," the man growled as he walked past her and over the hill toward Ki.

Ginger ran after him, feeling small and like a child. She followed behind the last few yards as if she were an obedient sheepdog.

The craggy old mountain man knelt beside the samurai and pulled up his sleeve to look at the infected arm before he examined the infected leg.

"Will he live?"

"Dunno," the giant said, scooping Ki up as if he were a big rag doll and tossing him over shoulders humped like those of a bull buffalo.

"Where are you going with him!" Ginger exclaimed, grabbing up the reins of her horse and scrambling into the saddle.

"Gonna try and mend him," Ben said. "You go on to Prescott, woman."

"No."

The giant turned. She thought he was going to shoot her dead or something, but he didn't. Instead, he just scratched his beard and said, "Go where you want. Just go and don't follow my flock."

"I'm coming with you and Ki."

"Your choice," he growled after a long moment's consideration. "Come along, then."

Ginger followed the man, and she was amazed at how much ground Ben Rodgers could cover with his huge strides, even carrying the weight of Ki. He went up a mountain without slowing down, and then he went down the other side even faster. Sometimes, as the morning passed away, he would stop at the crest of a ridge and stand frozen for several minutes as his eyes surveyed the country, missing nothing. Once he sharply warned her not to sky-light herself on horseback, but to stay below the ridgeline.

Ginger did not give him cause to speak harshly to her again on that point, and by midafternoon, with her horse stumbling with fatigue and starting to limp from the bare foot, she was wondering if Ben Rodgers would ever tire or reach whatever destination he sought.

Late afternoon found the man moving up a mountain stream so that he could not be tracked, and shortly before dark, he came to a large and very rustic log cabin hidden in trees just beyond a meadow. Hidden so well behind wil-lows and bushes that she would have walked by it without noticing, if it were not for the passel of puppies that came racing out to greet them. The puppies ignored her, but wagging their tails happily, they reared up against Ben's trunklike legs. The giant smiled and reached down to pat each one on the head before he pushed the cabin door open and vanished inside.

Ginger remained in the yard, unsure of what she should do next. The sun was setting over the western mountain-tops, and the air was taking on a chill. She thought she heard voices inside, and then she was astonished to see a tall, dignified Mexican woman appear in the doorway. The woman also wore buckskins, and although she was proba-bly in her early fifties, she was very attractive.

The woman smiled shyly, and in very slow and precise English, she said, "Please come into our *casa*, Miss Brown."

Ginger almost fell over backward. "Who are you!" she blurted.

"I am Maria Margarita Escobar Lopez Santiago," she

said, wiping her hands on her apron. "And I hope you like rabbit stew."

"I am famished!" Ginger took a step forward, then stopped in her tracks. "But what about my sick friend?"

Maria's smile died. "I do not know if we can save him. It is in God's hands and also the medicines that the forest gives us through God's work."

The Mexican woman made the sign of the cross and beckoned Ginger inside. The cabin was spotlessly clean, and it even had wooden floors. Everywhere she looked, Ginger saw the hands of a real craftsman. There were beautifully carved chairs, a massive bed, a chest, and even wooden plates, glasses, knifes, spoons, and forks on a huge pine table.

Ki was resting on the bed, and Ben was gone.

"He went to get some medicine," Maria said as she added wood to her rock fireplace and set a pot of water to boil. "He will be back very soon."

"I thought that he lived all alone," she said, finding it difficult to accept that Ben was not the haunted, blood-thirsty loner that everyone imagined.

"No," she said. "We have been together for fifteen years now."

Ginger could not help but smile. "I am glad," she told the woman. "I never liked the thought of someone being alone."

"He was never alone. Even before I came to him," Maria said. "All the creatures of the forest, they are his friends. He loves the sheep and the dogs. He was never alone, Miss Brown."

"How did you know my name?"

"My husband knew your father. He remembers you as a child."

Ginger heaved a heavy sigh. "That seems like a lifetime

ago. I'm afraid I have lost all my innocence, and I'm not the girl he remembers."

"You are a beautiful woman now, and you are the enemy of Jake Hammer. That makes you our friend. You are also Mando Santiago's friend. So you are good. Sit down. You will eat."

Ginger looked at Ki. "I can't eat with him sick."

"He will not get better if you starve. *Comprende?* Eat now. Please."

Ginger sat down, and when her plate was filled with stew, she ate.

It was long after dark when Ben returned with a gunnysack filled with wild herbs, leaves, roots, and even the bark from some tree. He dumped it all on the table, and then he and Maria quickly cut it up and then stuffed it into two pair of Ben's stockings. The stockings were thrown in the boiling water, and before they were hardly soaked, they were dropped on Ki's infected leg and arm.

The samurai's eyes flew open and a groan escaped his lips. He looked up at the giant and tried to reach for his knife, but Ginger's words stopped him. "No! They are friends."

Ki relaxed. "Then why are they burning my flesh?"

The giant said, "It's a poultice to suck out the poison. The dog that bit you, he wasn't frothin' at the mouth or anything, was he?"

"No," Ki said. "He wasn't that way."

"Good," Ben said with relief. "Otherwise, the best thing I could do for you would be to put a bullet through your head."

Ki swallowed. "I could use some water."

Ginger brought it to him and he drank, wondering where he was and who these people were that had taken him into their log cabin. He was just about to ask when two more steaming poultices replaced those that had already begun to cool.

Ki gritted his teeth and bit back a groan. His back arched and sweat erupted across his forehead.

The woman said, "We are sorry for this. If we had some whiskey, it would be easier. But my husband drank it all last Christmas."

"Sorry about that," Ben said. "Guess you're just gonna have to bite a stick or your tongue."

Ki wished he could use *atemi* on himself. This was an ordeal that he would just as soon have missed.

"This is Apache medicine," Ben said. "I learned it as a boy from Geronimo's grandfather."

"Has anyone died from the cure yet?"

"Not that I know of." Ben frowned. "You reckon that there will be a lot of men on your backtrail?"

"Yes," Ki said. "We rode up streams and tried to make it tough, but we only had the one horse, and I'm sure they'll follow us."

"Not from where I met you," the giant said. "Not unless they got an Apache tracker. But I can't take the chance that they might be comin'. If they want you bad enough, they'll fan out, and sooner or later they'll come here."

"I'm sorry this is causing you so much trouble."

"I was born for trouble. Trouble is all I know, mister. I tried to stay away from other men all my natural life, but they won't let a body be. They just hound him and hound him until he has to stand and fight 'em. Only friends I ever had were the Mexican sheepherders hereabouts. They was fair to me. Helped save my flock one winter when the snows got deeper than the roof of this cabin. I paid 'em back over the years as best I could."

"You repaid them a hundred times," Maria said.

She looked at Ki and Ginger. Her eyes showed pride and her chin was held high. "This one, he has killed more of Hammer's gunfighters than anyone knows. He saved many sheep and many sheeptenders from being ambushed. My people look at him as if he were . . . were their savior."

"Hell, Maria," Ben said. "Keep talkin' thataway and they'll think I'm the second comin' of the Lord!"

She scoffed at him. "Anyone who hears your language around the sheep will know that is not the way of it. But you are my family's hero. They will never be able to repay you. Nor can I."

Ben tried to hide his embarrassment, but failed. He changed poultices again, and Ki almost hit the roof. "How many of those are you going to apply?"

"As many as it takes to draw out the poison," Ben said. "Might take a day and a night."

"Then get your gun," Ki said.

But when Ben shrugged and got to his feet and walked over to his rifle, Ki added quickly, "I was only kidding!"

" 'Course you were," Ben said, with a slow wink. "But you needed to be reminded of the fact."

True to his word, the poultices kept coming, and after a while, the pain was less because the nerves seemed to have been fried. Ki sweat buckets, and Ginger kept sponging his brow with cool water. By morning everyone was exhausted, but the infected wounds were no longer filled with suppuration.

"You'll be fit again in a week," the giant said, taking up his rifle and heading for the door.

"Where are you going!" Maria asked, her eyes suddenly wide with fear.

Ben came back to her. "You rest easy in your mind. I got to go check on the flock and then pick up yesterday's

101

backtrail. Got to make sure that they're not coming here to pay us a visit."

"And if they are?"

"Then no one will be home," he said, kissing the woman's cheek. "Don't you worry. I'll be all right. Gotta feed those dogs that have been watching the flock all night. We've et. They need to do the same."

"Where did you send them?"

"Up on Baldy Mesa," he said, taking his rifle and pulling on a battered hat. "Mister, you ain't packing iron. Are you any good with a gun or a rifle?"

Ki raised his head. "I can shoot both," he said. "But I prefer a samurai's weapons."

"A what?"

"I'll explain later," Ginger said, looking to the giant. "I don't think you'd believe him anyway unless you saw him use them."

"Wagh," he grunted. "I guess that you're right."

Maria went to kiss her man good-bye, and then he was gone.

Ki looked up at Ginger. "I feel awful not being able to go with him. If he'd just have waited another few hours, maybe . . ."

She bent over and kissed him on the mouth. "Don't talk nonsense," she said. "You won't be fit to fight for a week at least. Besides, Ben Rodgers has been outfoxing and outfighting paid gunnies for as long as I can remember. He'll be all right."

Ki took a deep breath and closed his eyes. "I sure hope so," he said. "If we brought trouble to him . . ."

Ginger kissed him again, and this time Ki kept quiet. But all the rest of that day, as Maria and Ginger kept applying even more poultices—though he did manage to convince them they did not need to be so hot—everyone was tense.

"He *will* come back," Maria said again and again. "He always comes back."

"I'll be well enough to go after him tomorrow," Ki said.

"No, you won't," Maria said. "Don't talk crazy. Tell me about Mando."

"He was sentenced to life in prison," Ginger said. "They'll be taking him to the prison in Yuma. Probably today when the stage rolls through Alpine going west."

"He will never live to see the prison," Maria said gravely. "They will kill him on the road."

Ki and Ginger exchanged worried glances. It was exactly what Ginger had said the day before.

The samurai gnashed his teeth with impatience. He could not help Ben Rodgers or Mando. Ben would have to help himself, and maybe Jessie could save Mando.

For the moment at least, Ki had to face the truth that it was all out of his hands.

Chapter 11

It was midnight when the door to the marshal's office crashed open and Buck Timberman and Jake Hammer came barging inside.

"All right!" Hammer shouted. "Where the hell did your bloody samurai take Ginger Brown!"

"I haven't the slightest idea," Jessie said, rising from the plank she had been resting upon. "I've been locked up in here. How could I know what he is up to? And besides, I thought you said at Mando's trial—to use the word very loosely—that Ginger Brown had disappeared and no one knew where she was."

"Don't play games. You know where the samurai is and where he's taken the girl," Timberman snarled. "That yellow bastard works for you, don't he?"

Jessie stiffened. "If you are referring to Ki, then yes, he does. But again, I've been locked up in here, and I don't see how you can accuse me of knowing what the man is up to."

"You think you're real cute, don't you?" Hammer said in a sarcastic voice as he gripped the cell bars. "Well, lady, as far as I'm concerned, you can play your little games until the cows come home, but it won't change anything. First thing tomorrow morning, Mando here will be on a stage with a deputy and one of my best gunmen. They're going to take him all the way to Yuma."

"I think I'd rather stay right here," Mando said, forcing a grin. "Company I'm with is bound to be a lot prettier than what I'd find in the Yuma Prison."

"It doesn't matter what you want," Hammer replied. "You're prison bound and nothing will change that."

The cattle baron swung back on Jessie. "Your samurai killed one of my dogs last night and one of my men, too. He entered my house and kidnapped Ginger Brown, and then he stole a horse."

Hammer counted the offenses off one by one. "Murder. Kidnapping. Horse stealing. Every one of them is a hanging offense."

"My, my," Jessie clucked. "That does sound terrible. If I ever see him again, I'll have to reprimand him severely."

Hammer lunged at the bars, his fist reaching out. "You're pushing me too far, damn you!"

Timberman grabbed him and dragged him back from the cell. "Mr. Hammer! Get ahold of yourself!"

The marshal was a good four inches taller and fifty pounds heavier than the cattleman, and he held him until Hammer settled down.

"Let go of me, Marshal!"

Timberman released him, saying, "Why don't you go ahead and keep searching for the Chinaman and the girl? I'll stick around here until that stage comes through."

Hammer relaxed. "Okay."

"But what about the woman?"

Hammer frowned. "Turn her loose."

"Turn her loose?" Timberman did not understand.

"That's right." Hammer looked at Jessie. "Maybe you'll lead us to the samurai."

"Not very likely."

Hammer grinned with confidence. "We'll see about that. But it doesn't matter. I've got an Apache tracker on their trail. Ki and Ginger are riding one horse, so they can't get too far ahead before my men overtake them. Maybe you'd like to stay around Alpine to see your Chinaman sentenced and hanged? We work pretty fast here. Judge Larson doesn't believe in giving killers, kidnappers, or horse thieves much time before they swing."

Jessie said nothing.

Hammer smiled triumphantly at her, then barged out the door.

"Starbuck, best thing you can do," Timberman said, "is to take the next stage going toward Texas and never look back."

"I'll think about it," Jessie said. "When do I get out?"

"If you want out now, then I'll let you go," the marshal said. "I just thought that, seeing as how you like Mexican sheepmen so much, you might want to finish out the night with Mando."

Timberman laughed at his own crude sense of humor and held up the cell key. "Well, what's it to be?"

"I'll stay until morning," Jessie said.

"Ha! I had it figured right, didn't I!"

"Shut up," Mando said in a hard voice.

Timberman's eyes blazed with anger. "Mexican, you're going to be sorry you ever crossed me or Mr. Hammer. You're going to pay for it."

"With my life?" Mando stepped forward. "That's what you've got planned with Hammer, isn't it? I'll never reach Yuma."

The anger flooded out of the marshal. "You'll get there

unless there's some accident," Timberman said a little smugly. "Nobody can predict an accident."

"It won't be an accident," Mando said. "It'll be murder."

Timberman just shrugged his broad shoulders, then turned and went to the door. He whistled, and a few minutes later his deputy appeared. The deputy's name was George, and he was a short, pimply-faced man in his early twenties. George had a swagger and a way of talking out of the side of his mouth. He probably had not bathed in several months, and he stank worse than rotting fish.

Around town, George was actually known as "the Fish," but he was also grudgingly recognized as being an expert shot and faster on the trigger even than Timberman.

"What's up?" George said, glancing at the cell and resting his eyes on Jessie. "She gonna be set free tonight?"

"She decided to stay the night," Timberman said.

"You mean Mr. Hammer gave her the chance to get out of there and she wanted to stay?" George looked appalled.

"Yeah. And I want you to stay here while I go over to the house and catch a few winks before the morning stage rolls in. I'll be out in the hills all day tomorrow hunting that damn samurai if the Apache don't find him first. You'll be taking Mando out of here tomorrow."

"Sure," George said with a wink. "It'll be a pleasure. By the way, who's Mr. Hammer sending with me?"

"Ed Bates. But you're the deputy. You'll be the one in charge."

George grinned. "Then I'll call the shots," he said. "Just as long as Ed understands that."

"He does," Timberman said. "Just don't mess this up."

"Not a chance."

Mando said, "You can cut the act. I can guess that they'll kill me before I reach Yuma."

Timberman didn't bother to deny the charge. "George, you just watch them good because Mr. Hammer is on the warpath. If he comes ranting and raving in here asking for me, tell him I joined the search for the samurai."

"And if he don't believe me?"

"Make something else up," Timberman said. "Just keep an eye on the two of 'em until morning. I'll be here when the stage comes around to the front."

George nodded and when the marshal left, he plopped down in the officer's leather chair, put his feet up on the desk, leaned back, and tipped his hat down over his eyes before saying, "Don't interrupt my beauty sleep if you start screwin'."

Mando grabbed the bars and shook them with all his might, but Jessie didn't even give George the benefit of her anger. A few minutes later the deputy was snoring away peacefully.

Mando slumped down against the wall and massaged his temples. "They know how to make a man say things that he should not say."

Jessie sat down beside him. "You really think they intend to kill you on the way to Yuma?"

"Ain't any doubt about it," Mando said.

Jessie got up and began to pace back and forth. "Then I've got to figure out a way to stop them first."

"There is no way," Mando said. "It is not the first time that a prisoner has been shot after an 'attempted escape.'"

"I'll think of something," Jessie vowed.

Early the next morning a stage rolled up before the marshal's office. Minutes later, Timberman and his deputy drew their guns and opened the cell door.

"Time to go," the marshal said. "Put your hands behind

your back, cross your wrists, and turn around, or I'll pistol-whip you."

Mando knew better than to argue, and Timberman fastened the handcuffs on securely.

Timberman gave Mando a hard shove toward the front door. "Deputy, help the prisoner up into the stage and keep your gun on him. Bates is already inside and waiting."

George prodded Mando with his Colt. "Make one wrong move and you'll save us the trouble of leaving Alpine."

Jessie watched as Mando was hurried out the door. "How soon does the stage leave?" she asked.

"As soon as they can change and get a fresh team," the marshal answered. "You take my advice and get the next stage out, and when you get to Texas, don't even think about sheep or the Mogollon."

Jessie shoved past him and through the door. She walked directly over to the stage office two doors down the street and pulled a twenty-dollar bill out of her dress. "I want a ticket on that stage."

The man in charge blinked. "But Miss Starbuck," he said. "That's the wrong stage! It's going west. You want one that's going east."

"Wrong," Jessie said. "How much is a ticket?"

"But I can't sell you a ticket on that stage! That Mando Santiago is being taken to Yuma by a pair of deputies!"

"It's a public conveyance," Jessie said. "And if you don't sell me a ticket, I guess I'll just write a letter to your company's president. It'll be a strongly worded letter, and it won't do a thing for your future with this company."

Jessie paused just long enough to let the man digest what she had told him, then added, "How much?"

"How far?"

"To Yuma, if that's what it takes," she said.

The man gulped and sold her a ticket for $8.25, and Jessie pocketed her change. In about one minute some men outside were going to have a real shock.

She was very much looking forward to seeing their faces.

Chapter 12

Jessie walked out of the stage office with her ticket in her hand. She had a valise packed, and she was ready to leave.

"Hey!" Timberman challenged as she handed her ticket to the driver. "What the hell do you think you're doing?"

"Boarding this public stage for Yuma," she said, giving the big marshal a smile. "Anything wrong with that?"

"You can't ride this coach! You know damn good and well it's being used to transport Mando Santiago to prison."

"So what?" Jessie's green eyes flashed. "Marshal, Jake Hammer may own Alpine and all its officials, but he doesn't own this stage line. I've bought my ticket and I'm leaving. I'd strongly suggest that you do not interfere."

His cheeks colored red. "Miss Starbuck," he said in a voice that shook with rage, "if you get on that stage, I will not be responsible for what happens to you. Mando is a killer, and he just might try and escape. If he does, my deputies will gun him down, and you just might catch a stray bullet. Am I making myself very clear?"

"You couldn't have put it any plainer," Jessie said, pushing past the man and opening the door.

"Hey!" George squawked when the deputy saw her. "What do you think you're doing!"

"I'm going to Yuma," Jessie said, climbing up and taking a seat opposite Mando.

George started to grab her, but Timberman stuck his big head inside the coach and said, "Let her be. You men will just have to take care of the lady, same as you take care of Mando. Understood?"

Ed Bates nodded. "Be a pleasure, Marshal."

But George wasn't a bit happy. "Ain't no place for a lady to be," he groused. "Ain't right she should come along."

"Well, I am coming!" Jessie said. "So why don't you sit back and let's enjoy the trip."

"Jessie," Mando said. "I wish I could change your mind. Someone is gonna get shot before we reach Yuma."

"Don't you start in, too," she replied, turning her face away and looking out the window.

The stage pulled out of the station, and Jessie slipped her hand into her skirt to feel the comfort of her two-shot derringer. She had no idea where they planned to kill Mando, but she figured that it would not be long before they acted. Ed Bates was supposed to be Hammer's fastest gunman, and Timberman would want his deputy back as soon as possible.

Tonight, Jessie thought, with a sudden flash of intuition. They will try to kill him tonight at a stage stop.

The stage road followed the Salt River down its steep and twisted course off the western slopes of the Mogollon Rim. They met few eastbound wagons, and when they did, the road was so narrow that it was a hazard because the

112

downside was usually a chasm hundreds of feet deep. Just to look over the edge was unnerving, and on more than one occasion they all felt a wheel slip dangerously close to the edge.

By late afternoon everyone in the coach was worn down from nerves and suffering from lack of food and water.

Ed Bates was especially vocal. "When is that sonofa-bitchin' driver going to stop this thing for a meal!"

"There's a stage stop at the bottom where he'll change teams and we'll lay over for an hour or two," George said.

"I'll tell you this," Bates vowed. "I'm not riding a stage up this mountainside comin' back."

"What are you going to do?" George challenged. "Walk back to Alpine?"

"If I have to. But I figure to buy, steal, or borrow a saddle horse," Bates vowed. "I got some spending money. Mr. Hammer, he pays a lot more for his top people than a deputy makes, that's for damn sure."

"I ain't complaining," George replied. "I like my job just fine."

"Don't seem like much of a job to me," Bates said. "I got one boss, but you got two."

George scowled. "Well, that might change someday."

Jessie and Mando exchanged questioning glances. It was clear that the two men did not like each other. Maybe that could be used somehow to outwit them.

"Station comin' up!" the driver yelled. "Everybody prepare to get out."

When the stage rolled into the station ten minutes later, the sun was slipping toward the western horizon. But now that they were down at desert level, the air was hotter than it had been up on the rim, and Jessie saw that the horses were heavily lathered.

She dismounted without help and stepped aside as

George and Bates pulled Mando roughly out of the coach, shoving him hard enough to make him spill in the dirt.

"Get up, greaser!" Bates swore, grabbing Mando and dragging him to his feet, then backhanding him across the mouth.

Mando slammed up against the wheel of the wagon, and even though his hands were cuffed behind his back, he managed to drive the pointed toe of his riding boot up between Bates's legs. It was a tremendously powerful kick. It sounded like the impact the back feet of a mule would make when it kicked another animal, and it lifted Bates completely off the ground.

"Ahhh!" Bates screamed, grabbing his testicles and pitching to the ground to roll around in agony.

Jessie saw George double up his fist, and that's when she pulled the derringer out of her skirt and cocked it. "Freeze!" she yelled.

George spun around, his hand dropping for his sixgun before Jessie's green eyes told him she meant business and she'd kill him if he tried to clear leather.

"Goddamn you!" George cried in a rage. "I knew you'd try to mess us up!"

"Reach cross your belly with your left hand and throw your gun in the dirt!"

George shivered uncontrollably, but did as he was told. Jessie took the gun and said, "Now, unlock the handcuffs."

"No!"

"Unlock them or I'll shatter your kneecap, and you'll limp the rest of your days," she said.

George unlocked the handcuffs and Mando disarmed Bates, then cocked the gunman's Colt and said, "You have killed many of my people. I think now I will kill you."

"Mando!" Jessie protested loudly. "If you kill him,

there's nothing I can do to save you from prison or the gallows."

Mando didn't seem to hear her. He cocked the sixgun and placed its barrel right between Bates's eyes. "I think it would be worth going to the gallows to see your brains leak into the dirt."

Bates swallowed and shook his head. "Please," he begged. "Everything I done was just on orders. I never killed anybody that Jake Hammer didn't want killed. I swear it!"

"Shut up!" George shrieked. "You goddamn lily-livered coward, shut up!"

But Ed Bates, staring up into the merciless eyes of Mando Santiago, found he could not shut up. "I swear I never killed except under orders."

"I think," Jessie said, "that the territorial governor in Prescott might like to hear that."

Jessie saw a movement out of the corner of her eye. It was the stagecoach driver, and he had a shotgun clenched in his fists. "Drop the gun!" he rumbled.

"Don't do it," Mando warned, backing away from Jessie so that she would not take a blast if the man pulled the trigger.

It was an explosive and unusual kind of standoff. Jessie had her gun pointed at Bates. George was disarmed, and Mando now had a Colt revolver trained on the stagecoach driver, whose double-barreled shotgun looked menacing enough to blow them all to smithereens.

Jessie took a deep breath and appraised the situation coolly. Bates was still clutching his testicles and half-paralyzed with pain. He was not going to be a factor. George, unarmed, was just a little boy playing a man's game. The driver was the joker in the deck. He might work for Jake Hammer, but it seemed unlikely.

"Driver," she said. "This is not your affair."

"I'm responsible for my passengers," he argued.

"You heard what that man said about killing under Jake Hammer's orders."

"That ain't my concern one way or the other, lady. Now, you drop that sixgun and tell the prisoner to do the same."

"We can't," Jessie said simply. "They'd kill us in the bat of an eye if we did that."

"And I'll blow you apart if you don't," the driver said. "I mean it!"

Jessie now understood she was dealing with a simple man who was trying to do his job but was incapable of sorting out the complications and being reasonable.

"Listen," she said. "You can't kill both Mando and me. One of us will get you for sure."

"I didn't deal into this game," the driver said, licking his lips nervously. "But this shotgun gives me the best hand, and I'll bet that prisoner don't want his innards scattered all over the side of my stage."

"They'll be no winners if you pull the trigger," Jessie said. "Mando is going to prison for life. He's got nothing left to lose."

"That's right," Mando said. "And besides, you heard the man admit to killing my people under Jake Hammer's orders."

"Like I said, that ain't my concern. I don't want no part of any of this."

"Then start backing up toward the station," Jessie said. "Just keep backing up and don't interfere."

"Shoot 'em!" George cried. "Goddammit, driver, you got the scattergun, shoot 'em!"

But the driver looked at the gun in Mando's hand and how it was rock-steady, and then his eyes flicked to the derringer that Jessie had pointed at him, and he slowly

116

shook his head. "I got a wife and two kids," he said, backing toward the stage. "I got responsibilities to think of."

Jessie waited until the driver had vanished into the stage station, and then she said, "All right, Mando, do you know how to change the team?"

"No," he said. "I'm a sheepman. Remember?"

"Don't ask me to do it!" George snapped. "And Bates sure as hell can't after you almost kicked his balls off."

Jessie expelled a deep sigh. It had just occurred to her that the best thing to do would be to have a fresh team harnessed up and then to have the driver deliver them all to Prescott.

"I'd better go into the station and get some help," Jessie said, starting to turn.

"No!" Mando shouted, suddenly throwing himself at her as the driver opened up with both barrels of his shotgun from the station's doorway.

Mando's body caught the outer edge of the double patter of shot. Jessie felt him stiffen and then the sixgun bucked in his hand twice.

The driver jumped back out of the doorway, and Mando staggered to his feet. "We've got to get out of here!" he gritted. "Come on!"

Jessie knew that the driver would have his shotgun reloaded in seconds, and the next time he fired, he might be more accurate. As it was, Mando's shirt was already soaked with blood. As for George and Ed Bates, she could either kill them in cold blood or wash her hands of them for now.

"Come on!" Mando yelled, grabbing her and dragging her around behind the coach as George, followed by a bent-over Ed Bates, ran to the station.

"We've got to get out of here," Jessie said. "There are bound to be more weapons inside that station."

Mando agreed. "Get in!" he cried, leaping up to the driver's seat, unwrapping the lines and lashing them against the horses' sweaty backs.

The stage's wheels skewed wildly across the yard. Mando didn't know how to drive, but fortunately, the horses knew how to run.

Jessie saw George come racing out of the station with a gun in his fist. He was screaming, and as the stage almost flipped, the deputy opened fire on Mando.

Jessie fired both barrels of her derringer, and George threw himself on the ground.

A moment later they were racing out of control down the long, dusty road toward Yuma. Jessie supposed that there was a fork branching to the north toward Prescott, but without Ed Bates's confession of wrongdoing, there wasn't much point in looking up the governor anyway.

She sagged back in the seat and reloaded the derringer. Things had not worked out as well as she'd hoped. But on the other hand, they were alive and running free.

Things could have been worse, but then again, when George and Bates either saddled the station's fresh horse or harnessed it to a wagon, things probably would get worse in a hell of a big hurry.

Chapter 13

Mando pulled the exhausted team to a standstill about two miles east of the station where the road crossed a shallow stream. He wrapped the lines around the brake, then climbed unsteadily down to the road, and Jessie helped him over to a rock.

"Let me get that shirt off your back and let's see how badly you're wounded," she said.

The shirt was already starting to stick to Mando's back, and Jessie had a few bad moments pulling it away.

"I don't think it's as bad as it looks or feels," he said.

Jessie wet a strip of cloth in the stream and washed away the blood. "Looks like you were hit with about five shots up near the point of your shoulder. They need to be extracted and the wounds cleansed with disinfectant."

"There's no time," Mando said, looking into her eyes. "You know that George and Ed will be on our backtrail in a few minutes."

"Yes," Jessie said. "But we could make a stand right here."

"Yeah," Mando said. "But since they'll probably have at

119

least a couple of rifles and we don't have a one, I don't think that would work out too well. Both men are expert shots. They're professionals, and they won't make any dumb mistakes."

"Are you strong enough to ride?"

"Sure I am," Mando said. "But where to? I can't go back to Alpine."

Jessie expelled a deep breath. "Maybe I can exert a little influence and get you placed under protective custody at the capitol in Prescott."

"Uh-uh," Mando said, shaking his head. "I've seen enough jails. I just don't trust politicians. Nor judges or constables. Maybe I'll strike out for Mexico. I got friends down there. I could mend and . . ."

"And what?" Jessie said pointedly. "By the time you returned, your family would be beaten and so would the other sheepherders."

Mando stood up. He squinted out at the vast desert to the west of them and shook his head. "So maybe I ought to go back to Alpine after all. If I could kill Jake Hammer, that would solve everything. He's the one that's pulling all the strings."

"Yes," Jessie said. "He is. But there are other cattlemen involved. Even if you somehow did find a way to reach and kill Hammer, someone would take his place unless that whole group is broken and the law comes down hard enough to see that everyone's rights are protected on the Mogollon."

"So what's the answer!" Mando demanded with exasperation.

"The answer is to get the public officials in Prescott to wake up to what's happening around Alpine. I can do that with your help."

"They won't believe a Mexican. Especially a sheep-ranching Mexican."

Jessie went over to the team of horses. "You have a knife, Mando?"

"Sure."

"Then let's cut these horses free and ride the two best ones for Prescott."

"Didn't you hear what I just told you?"

"Yes. You said they wouldn't believe a Mexican. Well, I just happen to think I can make them believe you, Mando. But you have to help me."

"I would rather ride back to Alpine and kill Hammer," he said stubbornly.

Jessie sighed. "Of course you would. But that wouldn't end it. You'd be gunned down or hanged. Your people would be accused of being a pack of murderers, and they'd lose the Spanish land grants that they have enjoyed and protected for generations. Is it worth seeing them all lose so that you can have your sweet revenge?"

Mando ground his teeth. In reply, he reached for his knife and began cutting the horses free. "We will take these two," he said. "To Prescott."

Jessie smiled. "Those are the ones I'd have picked, too," she said. "I just hope you can ride bareback and not fall off."

Mando scoffed. "I can ride like an Indian," he said. "You are the one that should worry."

Jessie smiled and climbed into the coach, where she changed into a pair of man's Levi's and a cotton shirt. She buckled her well-oiled sixgun around her shapely hip and lamented the fact that she had forgotten to bring a hat to shield her eyes from the sun's glare.

But the sun was setting now, and with any luck at all, they would be in Prescott by late tomorrow. If the horses

121

stood up to the trail, and if Bates and George did not overtake them on fresh horses and then kill them with the superior firepower of rifles.

It was a long, hard night of riding over country that they were not familiar with. They used the North Star to guide them in the general direction they figured Prescott would be, but they kept running into box canyons and having their progress blocked by deep ravines.

By dawn their horses were played out, and they had not traveled more than twenty-five miles. Jessie and Mando rode up near the crest of a summit and dismounted. They tied their horses in a copse of manzanita and slowly crawled up to study their backtrail.

"There they are," Mando said, pointing to a place where the two riders had dismounted and were studying their tracks.

Jessie watched Ed and George lead their horses across a rocky escarpment and then remount. They were not more than an hour behind.

"Their horses are fresh," she said. "Ours are finished. I don't think running is the answer."

"No," Mando said quietly. "We have no choice but to ambush and finish them. We won't reach Prescott any other way."

"I want to take them alive if possible," she said.

"Why?"

"Because Ed Bates will confess about what is going on in Alpine if he's forced to," Jessie said. "He'll sing like a bird to the governor and the politicians, which is exactly what we need."

"The deputy won't confess anything," Mando said. "He's too proud. He would rather die than betray his boss.

And just remember this—they won't be planning on taking us alive."

"I know that," Jessie said. "But we still have to give them a chance to surrender. I won't have them gunned down in cold blood."

"Then let's find a place to spring a trap," Mando said.

Jessie nodded and slipped back down from the summit, then went to her horse. Because it was a draft animal, it was huge and powerful but slow. Riding the beast all night bareback had been an agony because of the width of its back and the uncomfortableness of its lumbering gait. And after helping to pull the stage all the way from Alpine and then having to go another full night through tough country, the poor beast was finished. Its legs, chest, and shoulders were torn by the brush that it had been forced to make headway through in the darkness, and its mane and tail were tangled with stickers.

"Wish I had a bucket of grain to feed you," Jessie said, patting the animal's muscular neck. "But I don't. All I can say is that the running is over."

"Almost," Mando said, grabbing a fistful of mane and swinging onto the animal's back. "We might still have to go another mile or two before we find a place to make our stand."

Jessie led the tall draft horse over to a rock, which she hopped onto and then mounted the horse. The bridles and reins they'd fashioned from harness were crude, but effective.

"Come on, horse," she said. "Not much farther."

Ten minutes later Mando pulled up under a cluster of big rocks. He shaded his eyes and looked up at them. "What do you think about catching them by surprise from up on top?"

"I think that'll do fine," Jessie said, riding her horse around the rocks and dismounting.

They tied their horses behind the rocks and climbed up them until they had a vantage point about ten feet over the trail below.

"What do you think now?" Jessie asked.

"I'd rather not jump them," Mando said before he added, "Is that what you had in mind?"

Jessie looked down. From below, the rocks had not seemed very tall, but from up on top ... well, it seemed like a long way down. "Let's just get the drop on them."

Jessie and Mando waited almost an hour before they heard the sound of iron horseshoes striking rock.

"Here they come," Mando said.

The two riders came into view. George was riding slightly ahead, his eyes trained downward on the tracks he followed. Ed Bates rode off to his right, his eyes swiveling back and forth across the trail as if he were expecting an ambush and not wanting to be the first one to ride into someone's gunsights.

When they were almost directly underneath, Jessie said, "Hold up, both of you!"

George's head snapped up as his hand went down to the gun on his hip. He was extraordinarily fast, but also foolish. Jessie and Mando both fired simultaneously, and their bullets smashed down through the young deputy's shoulder and pierced his heart and lungs. George died instantly, and when he fell, his horse, a fine roan, stampeded off into the brush just as Bates sank spurs into his horse's flanks in a desperate attempt to get away.

Mando came flying off the rock like a sleek cougar. One moment he was flat on his stomach, the next he was leaping through the air. His outstretched fingers caught Bates by the neck and ripped him from the saddle. Both men fell hard, but it was Mando who sprang to his feet and whose fist smashed into the point of his opponent's jaw, sending him backpeddling.

Bates was taller than Mando, but thin. His hand flashed down to his gun, but Mando was on him too fast. The sheep rancher chopped down the edge of his hand and knocked the gun spinning. Bates took three punches in the face, then dug under his coat and pulled a knife.

"So," Mando said. "Is that how it is to be?"

"Any way you want it, greaser!"

Bates's face was ugly with hatred as he lunged at the shorter man.

Mando jumped back, and when the arm and knife sliced past his belly, he drove his own blade into Bates's side, then twisted it.

Jessie saw the gunman's mouth fly open and his eyes bulge. She looked away, and when she heard the sound of falling rocks and breaking brush, she looked again to see Mando standing beside the edge of the trail. Ed Bates was nowhere to be seen.

"He's dead," Mando told her. "I tried to guide my hand differently so that my steel did not find its way toward his heart. But I couldn't. I was taught from childhood that, when a man tries to kill you, you must try to kill him."

Mando shrugged his shoulders. "I am sorry."

Jessie nodded. "You were fighting on instinct and for your life. If you had taken the time to think instead of react, it might have been you who had been killed in that fight."

Jessie climbed down from the rock and came to stand beside Mando. "It's just that now we have no confession against Jake Hammer and his bunch," she said.

"There are many others," Mando said. "Alpine is full of gunmen hired by Jake Hammer to kill my people."

Mando swayed and reached for Jessie.

"Are you all right?" she asked suddenly. "Did he stab you . . ."

"No. I am all right."

But despite his assurances, Mando kept leaning on her and trying to steady himself. "I guess I'm not quite up to snuff," he said wearily.

"We both need food and rest," she said. "Remember that abandoned log cabin we passed a few miles back?"

"Yes."

"Let's spend a day and a night there. Maybe, if you're up to it, I can dig those shot out of your back, and then I can hunt a deer or at least some rabbit."

Mando nodded weakly. "That's the best idea I've heard in a long time," he said.

The cabin was not abandoned, only temporarily unused. The door had been wedged shut as a protection against racoons and other mischievous raiders, and Jessie had to climb through the window covered with buckskin. But once she aired and swept the place out, it was comfortable. There was even a stack of firewood out back, and Jessie built a fire and then shot a pair of cottontail rabbits in a small meadow not far away.

"Before we eat, I've got to get that shot out of your back, or you're going to get lead poisoning," she told Mando.

"I figured you had that in mind when you put that water to boil." He scowled. "All right. Let's get it over with."

Jessie brought the pot of boiling water over, then used Mando's own knife to dig the shot out of his flesh. Only one of them was very deep. "This one is the last and the worst," she said. "So hold steady."

"You're doing just fine. As good as any doctor could,"

126

he hissed between clenched teeth as he lay stretched out on a bunk. "Just finish it up."

"I will. But it sure would help if I had forceps."

Jessie frowned in concentration. She slipped the knife blade in deep until she felt the tip strike the hard piece of shot. She could feel Mando's entire body stiffening, and she could only imagine how much it must have hurt the man, though he didn't make a sound.

"Almost done," she told him.

By pressing the fingernail of her index finger hard against the tip of her knife, she finally managed to pin the shot and roll it out of the wound. "There! Got it!"

Jessie cleansed the wound, which bled very little, and then bandaged it with an old washtowel that she took out of the boiling water and let cool for a few minutes.

"You're going to be good as new in the morning," she promised.

Mando reached up and touched her cheeks. "You are a savior," he said. "You help me escape, you fight at my side, you dig lead from my flesh, and then you cook me rabbit stew. Is there anything you cannot do?"

Jessie laughed out loud as much from relief to have the minor surgery finished as from his words. "There is plenty I cannot do."

"There is one other thing you could do for me," Mando said, his eyes dropping a little to her breasts. "But perhaps it is too much to ask."

Jessie had no trouble at all catching his meaning. She had seen him looking at her that way several times before, and so this was not a big surprise, although she was surprised at his timing. "After what you've just been through? Are you serious?"

"Perhaps I am serious *because* of what we have just

been through. You saved my life. This makes you a part of me, and I a part of you."

Jessie's eyebrows raised. "How do you figure?"

"It is just that way," he said, as if that explained everything.

Before Jessie could tell him that his words sounded to her like nonsense, Mando's lips were against hers and he was pulling her body close. His kiss aroused a fire in Jessie that she had not enjoyed for quite some time, and she found that she did not want him to stop.

Mando broke their kiss, then unbuttoned her man's shirt and studied her bare breasts. "I did not think you were wearing anything under the shirt," he said with a wide, handsome grin. "And that has been driving me crazy."

Jessie smiled. "I'd have thought that you were in such a fix that all you could think of would be how to escape."

"I know," he said. "That is what I should have been thinking about, but when I looked across the coach at these, all practical thoughts left my mind."

Mando's mouth covered one of Jessie's full breasts, and she closed her eyes and enjoyed the sweet sensations right down to her toes. He laved her nipples until they grew hard, and then he unbuckled her gunbelt and then her pants.

"If the rest of you is as beautiful as this part," he said, kissing each breast with reverence, "then heaven holds no greater promises for a poor sheepman."

Jessie said nothing, but when he peeled her boots, pants, and undergarments away to strip her bare, she could see the wonder of his appreciation. His strong brown hands pulled her silken thighs apart and then he buried his face into her womanhood, sending her into shivering ecstasy.

Mando lifted her buttocks completely off the bed, and she could feel his tongue moving in and out of her body, his hot breath seeming to fuel the fires of her passion until she was moaning with desire and her hips were grinding shamelessly as he feasted like a starved animal on her wet honeypot.

"Stop," she pleaded after a long time, when she felt as if something inside of her was going to explode. "I can't . . . can't stand it any more. I want you now!"

Almost reluctantly he lowered her hips to the bed, then stood and undressed. He was brown and sleek, and Jessie reached for his long, dark root. She held it in her hands and felt it throb to the beat of his heart, and then she bent her legs wide apart and watched the look of pure joy on his face as he slipped his big rod into her.

"It is such a pleasure to wrap my legs around you rather than that big draft horse I had to ride last night," she breathed.

Mando laughed. "Are you sore?"

"Not after what you just did to me," she told him.

"Good," he panted. "I don't want you sore unless it is I, Mando Santiago, that makes you sore."

"It will take a lot to do that."

"I have a lot," he grunted, slamming his rod far up inside of her and watching her face as she moaned with a mixture of pleasure and sweet pain.

Again, their lips clashed and their tongues and bodies moved in and out of each other wetly. After several long minutes Jessie found that she was losing control. Her heels kept sliding up and down the outsides of Mando's legs, and her breath was coming fast.

"I'm going to come first," she whispered into his ear. "Just don't stop!"

He laughed and his narrow hips began to piston up and down very powerfully. Jessie bit her lower lip, and her fingernails bit into his buttocks, pulling him as deep as he could go until suddenly, her mouth flew open and she began to buck wildly, crying out unintelligibly as her body milked the man on top of her until he too, was out of control.

They came together. Jessie dimly felt his hot seed fill her hungry body as his body spasmed and then finally went limp.

For long, heart-pounding moments, they stayed locked in a lover's embrace until Mando rolled off of her and smiled.

"After dinner we will take more time," he said, his dark eyes still glazed with passion.

Jessie nodded and drew his face down to her breasts. "Yes," she panted, "we need to take lots more time."

★

Chapter 14

The craggy-faced giant stopped at the edge of Baldy Mesa and slipped down flat on his belly so that just the top of his head showed. In his massive fists he held a Model 1873 Winchester caliber .44-40. It carried fifteen rounds under a twenty-four-inch barrel and used the newer center-fire cartridges which contained forty grains of powder, enough to knock down a grizzly or kick a man clean off his horse.

For almost thirty minutes Ben Rodgers remained motionless. He felt the sweet breath of air on his cheeks, tasted the perfume of wild meadow flowers, and dimly listened to the bleating of his sheep.

His enemies were coming. He had seen the glint of a silver concho reflecting across the thin mountain air across a distance of perhaps eight miles.

A blue-haired dog, battle-scarred of muzzle and with one ear half chewed off, growled softly just behind him, and the giant reached out and scratched its head.

"Yeah, Old Scout, they've found my trail," Ben said. "And there is no way I can stop them from following right up to the base of this mesa. We're done for. There's just no way offa here except straight down that trail yonder, and they'd spot and catch us and the flock before we was half-way down."

The battle-scarred sheepdog whined softly as if commiserating with the situation.

"We'll just have to make a stand," Ben said. "Do the best we can to stop 'em from getting up here on top and having their way with us and the flock."

Ben frowned. He wondered if he was getting old and careless so that he could be tracked. Yesterday he had thought that putting his flock up on this big, high mesa was the smart thing to do because, unless a man knew the way up, he would ride around it never realizing that two thousand sheep were hidden just seven or eight hundred feet overhead.

But now Ben realized bringing the flock up on Baldy Mesa had been a colossal mistake. The posse that was tracking him must have employed an Apache. No white man could follow Ben's trail. No, sir! Not even when he was old and half blind in twenty or thirty years.

But an Apache could track a horsefly through a desert sandstorm. Ben decided that he must kill the Apache first, and then he would take as many of Jake Hammer's men out as he could before they got to him, the dogs, and his flock.

And they would get to them. Ben hadn't had time to count the opposition yet, but there were at least thirty men in that hunting party. Most of them would be professional killers, but others would be cattle ranchers and their cowboys who owed Jake a favor or two. They'd all be good men with a gun or rifle, and a few of them would probably have been smart enough to have packed some hefty firepower. Rifles that were far bigger and nastier than his faithful '73 Winchester.

"But I'll bet not a one of them knows this country like I

do or can shoot as long and as straight," Ben said to the dog.

The animal's tail slapped the dirt because it understood that Ben was talking hope and encouragement.

Another twenty minutes passed before the men on his backtrail halted in a clearing and Ben had a chance to get an accurate count. There were thirty-three riders.

Damn, Ben thought, quickly counting his shells and coming up with only fifty. He was not going to have a whole lot of extra lead to spare.

Ben edged back from the mesa and studied his flock of two-year-old ewes, almost all of whom had lambed in the spring. There was a good bunch of black ones among the white, and he'd already docked their tails and done the castrating. He and Maria had roasted, boiled, and fried lamb nuggets for nearly a month until they got too ripe to eat, and then he'd fed them to the dogs.

"I'm going to lose the whole durn bunch," Ben lamented. "Hammer's boys and his friends will battle their way up here and kill me and you, then they'll just stampede the flock over the edge, rimrockin' the whole damn lot of them. Ain't no other way it can go, Old Scout."

The dog licked his hand and whined again. It's eyes were sad and it sighed fitfully.

"But we'll make 'em pay," Ben said. "Yes, sir! Before it's over, there will be blood all over the trail leading up here and I'll use every damn one of these fifty shells!"

Ben pulled the extra shells out of a leather "possibles bag." The same bag that he'd used to carry powder and balls when he'd hunted and trapped for a living a long, long time ago.

He laid the shells out on a flat rock, arranging them neatly side by side in a line before he moved back down the slope and spoke to each of his dogs.

"Curly, you're a good-un," he said, rubbing a brown dog's back and making it twist with happiness. "And Bill, you're lazy, but the best coyote killer besides myself in these here mountains.

"Honey Bear, come on over here and let me scratch your belly a minute, girl! You're the mother," he told her. "You got to watch out for the flock and the boys. When the sheep go over the side, you and the boys that are left, you run like hell down the mountainside. You know that little game trail back of us. You run for that and don't stop until you get home. Hear me, girl?"

Honey Bear yipped and then she barked softly.

Ben and Old Scout walked through the flock, both man and dog looking at each ewe as if it were a person. A real good cattleman, maybe one with just a few thousand head, he probably knew every head on his place, too. How they walked and how they sounded. He could spot the sick ones at a glance, and he knew them better than people knew people.

"You girls . . ."

Ben did not finish because he couldn't summon up any words. Instead, he turned and headed back to his rifle and shells. The hunters ought to be getting close by now. In another fifteen or twenty minutes some of the leaders were going to start dying.

Ben sighted in on the squat Apache tracker. The man had kept looking up at the mesa, and he probably had guessed that the one he followed was waiting in ambush somewhere up on top. But what he did not believe was that anyone could kill him from such a distance, shooting downward at such an angle.

It was going to be a very difficult shot, and Ben took his time. His mind worked without conscious effort as the

134

sights of his gun measured and accounted for wind, eleva-
tion, angle, and distance. And then his finger slowly
squeezed the trigger of the Winchester, and it boomed with
authority.

Ben counted out loud, "One, two."

Suddenly the Apache's arms flew out wide, and he tot-
tered on the back of his speckled pony for an equal count,
then he crashed over as Ben levered and fired a second
shot.

A cattleman he vaguely remembered as being one of the
men who had killed Manuel Escalante three years ago, died
next to the Apache.

Two more shots and the posse was scattering. Ben managed to wing a third enemy before the rest vanished into
the brush and trees and then, tentatively at first, started to
return a scattered rifle fire.

Ben distained them for a few minutes, not even bothering to take cover until the first heavy bang of a Spencer
bracketed across the distance. He saw the big hunting
rifle's bullet ricochet off a rock some ten feet from him and
he smiled. The Spencer's owner was not a marksman. He'd
get closer as time passed, but he was not a marksman, and
if the bastard showed his head, he'd be one of the first to
get leaky brains.

For the next hour Ben spent his precious bullets like a
miser, and every shot either killed or wounded one of his
enemies.

But they were advancing. He could not help the fact.
There was just so much cover for them to use that it was
impossible to keep them from coming up the side of the
mesa. And when one advanced, the others created a withering fire so that Ben could not fire without getting riddled.

Ben looked up at the sun and judged it was still only
about three in the afternoon. It was too early for darkness

to save him. They'd be over the edge of the rim in another fifteen or twenty minutes. There were just too damn many of them still alive and too few bullets for his hot rifle.

Ben reloaded one last time. There was a momentary lull in the action and he looked back over his shoulders to see all of his dogs keeping the increasingly nervous flock under control.

His broad chest filled with pride for his brave and hard-working dogs. A man could always buy more sheep, but a good sheepdog was rarer than a good woman.

Maybe I should run to fight another day, he thought. Maybe I should try and get away.

It did make sense, but it twisted his guts even to think about abandoning his flock. Twisted his guts so tight up inside that he felt like he was going to choke.

A bullet struck him in the ear, and Ben instinctively grabbed for it only to discover the ear was gone. He roared with anger and shot the man who had shot him. He brought down two more, and they were coming fast now and less than a hundred yards below.

A second bullet spun him around, and he knew without even bothering to look that he'd been hit solidly in the shoulder. He bellowed a challenge at the men below and worked the lever of his rifle.

Ben slapped at his arm and saw a hole where another bullet had just passed through his fringed and beaded buck-skin shirt. A shirt that Maria had given him for Christmas one year and which he had prided her on expert workman-ship and the artistry of her design.

Old Scout whined and the sheep had started to mill and bleat in near panic.

"Damnation!" Ben swore, firing his last bullet. "I think I'll get the hell outa here to fight another time. I ain't ready to die yet."

He turned and ran, calling his dogs after him. He was not fast, but his legs were so long that he covered ground with remarkable swiftness for a man who had no spring left in his sinew.

He ran across the mesa with his dogs after him as bullets streaked after the lot of them. He did not have the courage to look back at the sheep he had raised and loved, so he just plunged over the far lip of the mesa, swearing and crying and cussing as he went down through the brush and the trees faster than it seemed a man could do without tumbling and breaking his neck.

He kept his footing and he kept the empty rifle clenched in his huge fist and his legs did not stop churning until he reached the bottom of the mesa. Bullets were still tracing after him, and when he looked back, he saw two dead sheepdogs, young ones just too proud and foolish to leave their charges. Ben saw them and he wept some more.

But then he saw something else that broke his heart. First one reluctant, bleating woolly came tumbling over the side of the mesa, then they came pouring over like a river of cotton balls. Only cotton balls didn't make horrible sounds or come apart on rocks, drenching them with bloodstains.

Ben choked and dropped to his knees as the torrent of sheep kept streaming over the edge. He closed his eyes and dropped his rifle to clamp his hands over his ears. But he could still hear the poor, dumb wollies flying out into space and then striking the rocks with a dull, sickening thud.

Old Scout and the other dogs whined and then howled as they bit into his bloodied shirt and pulled him under a low pine tree where he could not be reached by bullets.

And when the rimrocking was finished, they seemed to pull him on deeper into the forest. He had left behind his rifle and his wealth, but as he staggered on, he grew calmer and more deadly. He had killed their Apache tracker and more than one wealthy cattleman, hadn't he?

He had made them shed human blood for that of sheep, hadn't he also? And now they were hurt, and shamed. They'd come after him, of course. They had horses and there were bound to be a few men who could track, though none as well as the Apache. He would lead them in circles. Kill those that he could and strike fear into the hearts of the rest until they no longer wanted to hunt Ben Rodgers.

Ben stepped out in the open and raised his hands as if to the Lord. "Come on, you bloody bastards!" he yelled. "Catch me if you can! I'm old. I'm afoot. I'm out of bullets. Come on and catch me!"

In answer, a volley of rifle fire erupted from up on top of Baldy Mesa, and a cloud of white gunsmoke drifted against the backdrop of an azure, cloudless sky. But the firing distance was great, the angle difficult to gauge, and none of the bullets came close.

"Come and get old Ben Rodgers!" he shouted.

The men on Baldy Mesa stopped firing. Ben saw a few of them drag the last of his poor ewes over to the edge and hurl them over the side to watch them splatter on the rocks below.

"You bastards!" he screamed. "Come and get me! I got the girl and the samurai, too! Come and get us all!"

From up on top a huge man wearing a badge suddenly appeared, and Ben recognized him at once as being Buck Timberman.

"Surrender and give us the samurai and Miss Brown!" he yelled through cupped hands. "If you don't do it, we'll hunt you down and kill you!"

"You'll never catch me, Buck! This is my country. Not yours!"

There was a long moment of silence. "We'll catch you

all right. And if we don't, we'll kill off the Santiagos and then all the rest. We'll drive the whole damn bunch outa this country once and for all. You'll be so busy running, you won't be able to interfere."

Ben swallowed. He should have guessed that Timberman would come up with that kind of threat. It was his only hold.

But hell, if he surrendered, they'd just torture him for information, and then they'd hang or shoot him and the dogs whether or not he talked.

"Come on, Buck. Just you and me!" Ben shouted. "Like before, with our fists. Remember how that was!"

Timberman cursed and the sound of it echoed over the mountains and valleys. Ben laughed, for he knew that whipping the marshal had scarred the man forever.

"We'll get you!" Buck screeched. "We got another Apache coming to help, and we'll get you!"

Timberman and the others suddenly vanished, and Ben knew that they were running for their horses. They would have to hoof it down to the animals and then gallop all the way around the mesa. They'd not be able to reach this place for at least twenty minutes.

Ben shook his head and absently touched where the lower part of his ear was now missing.

He grinned murderously at his dogs. "I don't believe they got another Apache, or they'd already have been using him. So we're going to run them in circles like a bunch of damn rabbits.

"It'll be a merry and a dangerous chase. We can't let them suspect where the cabin might be, and we can never go near it until this is finished. We'll have to find food on the land and survive by our wits until I can kill one of them and get some more bullets."

The dogs barked and danced around him with excitement. Ben chuckled. "Old Scout, those sons and daughters of yours think this is going to be a real lark. They don't understand that we're gonna play a deadly game."

Old Scout wagged his tail with encouragement. Ben walked slowly up the mesa until he found his rifle. He used the fringes on his sleeve to wipe it off clean, and then he took a deep breath and studied the land around him which he knew better than a city man knew his own backyard.

Then, with the dogs in front of him and two thousand broken woollies lying behind him, he set up with his long, sure strike.

He knew a place where the ground was covered with lava rock. It was treacherous country for a horse because the sharp rocks would slice their feet and fetlocks to ribbons. The cowboys and cattlemen would hate it. And they'd hate him. In the lava bed country he'd take away the advantage of the horses. He'd make the men walk, and they weren't used to walking in their damned stupid high-heeled boots.

He'd lame them like he'd lame their horses, and then he'd get himself some more bullets and commence to whittling down the odds.

Chapter 15

Buck Timberman's face was still mottled with rage when he finally returned to the horses. "How many did you lose trying to get up on top?" he demanded.

"We lost eight white men and the Apache scout," a rancher named Dawson said, not looking at the marshal. "And two cowboys are bad wounded."

"Jeezus!" Buck swore. "You were supposed to wait for me before you closed!"

"We saw him up there and figured we had better get him kilt or he'd get away."

"Yeah!" Timberman surveyed the survivors. "Well, you didn't get him 'kilt,' and he still got away!"

The men finished reloading and checking their cinches. To a man, they wanted Ben Rodgers's hide. One of them, a cadaverous gunfighter named Mace Holligan, said, "It's a good thing you brought them new Apaches and those bloodhound dogs. That sheepman has got his dogs, and they'll leave plenty of scent to follow."

Everyone turned to look at the two new Apache scouts. They were, like the dead one, squat fellows. Dark, expressionless, and without muscular definition, everyone knew they were deceptively strong and absolutely tireless.

"We better get going before that old bastard reaches another county," Mace said.

Buck Timberman cleared his throat. "I'm taking the Apaches with me," he announced. "Mace, you got the bloodhounds."

"What!"

"You heard me."

Mace and the others were not pleased. Mace said, "What the hell are you going to be doing while we go after Rodgers?"

"Me and the Apache are going to be hunting for his place. I've heard it said he has a cabin and even a Mexican wife. If we capture them, even if you fail, we'll still have Ben. He'll come after his own woman. So, what I'm doing is insurance."

"Well, dammit!" one of the ranchers cussed. "So we've got to go after the mountain man and all you're going to be doing is hunting his cabin and his wife! And you got both Apache scouts! No, sir! I won't hear of that."

Timberman had expected resistance, and he was prepared to bargain. He didn't need both Apache, but had asked for them so that he could give back one and allow the posse to think it had struck a good bargain.

"All right," he said with resignation. "You got the dogs and one of the trackers. Mace, you're in charge. You don't come back without Rodgers. And if you do, Mr. Hammer said it had better be draped across your saddle. Same goes for the rest of you that have hired out your guns. You're being paid top wages, Mr. Hammer expects results, and those results better be Ben Rodgers's topnotch. Have I made it real clear?"

They all nodded. Even the cattlemen and cowboys who did not work for Jake Hammer. Satisfied, Buck mounted his horse.

"Well, what about the dead!" said the rancher named Dawson. "We can't just leave them for the buzzards."

Timberman looked down at the bodies. "You do whatever you want," he said. "As long as you do it in five minutes or less. They're dead. They can't be helped. But if you men fail to bring back Rodgers, God help us all."

"Go to hell!" a cattle rancher spat. "Two of them are my neighbors! I'm quitting this hunt and taking them back to their ranches."

"Suit yourself," Timberman said. "I'll tell Mr. Hammer that when the chips were down, you folded up your tent and ran."

"You tell him whatever the hell you want, Buck! I just don't give a damn."

The rancher looked at several other of his neighbors. "This whole business stinks! Look at us! We're nothing but a pack of wolves, and we got the living shit shot out of us today. Maybe it's time we ought to start using our heads to think with instead of jerk up and down whenever Jake Hammer asks us to do his dirty work. You don't see him riding beside us, do you!"

Buck stepped forward menacingly. "I think you'd better load up your friends and get them the hell outa here while you're still able to, Mr. Dawson. Seems to me you talk too much."

But Dawson did not back down, and when another rancher said, "I reckon I'll give you a hand," the other ranchers fell in behind him and their cowboys backed them in a hurry.

"All right," Buck said. "So we've winnowed out the

men from the boys. That's fine. So let's get the job done! Mace, you're in charge of finding and killing Ben Rodgers. I'll find his place and his woman. We'll meet in Alpine, and then we'll settle this once and for all."

Mace and the other professional gunmen mounted their horses.

"Hey, Mace!" Timberman yelled.

Mace, the Apache scout, and the others he was leading stopped, but their bloodhounds kept moving. "If you boys come across the samurai, kill him on sight. He's probably even more dangerous than old Ben Rodgers. You saw what he did when he got past the dogs and took Ginger out of Hammer's mansion."

Mace nodded. He understood perfectly.

Buck and his lone Apache stared south. It was just a hunch, but he figured that Ben Rodgers would get as far away from his own place as he could. And Ben had been going north.

Ben reached the lava rock country at sundown. He stared out at the bleak, treeless plain and shook his head. Unfortunately, his own moccasins were getting thin from hard use, and he knew that they would not last more than ten miles across this stuff before they'd be shredded.

But even more discouraging was the thought that his dogs would suffer as the pads of their feet were sliced by the sharp rocks. Ben pulled off his leather shirt and sat down on a rock. He quickly cut the shirt into many little squares and strips which he used to tie around the dogs' feet.

"There," he said to Bill. "Now you and your friends got moccasins same as me. Better, in fact, 'cause mine are most worn out."

144

Ben stood up. The men who followed him could not be far behind. Maybe five or six miles. If he did not move quickly, they would run him down before their horses went lame.

"Let's go," he said, starting across the sea of lava.

For a moment the dogs stared out at the inhospitable plain, and then they looked back up at their master. They were unhappy. Their sheep were gone, and without sheep their lives were incomplete.

"Come on!" he called.

The dogs started after Ben, goose-stepping awkwardly until they became accustomed to their new foot coverings.

Ben moved as fast as he could, but found he was tired. He carried some dried jerky in his pockets, but he did not want to use it until evening, when he'd share it with his dogs.

Sundown found him limping painfully through the lava fields but unwilling to halt long enough to repair his now ruined moccasins. He could faintly hear the bloodhounds far behind him, and whenever they howled, his own dogs would twist around and their hair would raise up on their backs as they growled.

"Don't worry about them," he said to Old Scout and the others. "They'll go lame pretty quick now, and they'll refuse to take up the hunt in the morning."

Ben greeted the sunset with joy in his heart, and the moment it became dark, he changed the course of his escape slightly to the east. It was near midnight when he finally came to a small spring and laid his weary carcass down beside his dogs.

"Here," he said, taking the jerky out of his pocket and dividing it up between the animals, saving an equal share for himself. "We'll sleep a couple of hours, and then we'll move along."

When Ben awoke, he realized that he had slept more than four hours. He pushed himself erect and stood very still for a long moment, and then he heard the cry of the bloodhounds, loud and distinct. The nearness of them made him stiffen with alarm.

"They're within a mile of us!"

Ben realized instantly that he had underestimated the men on his trail. Obviously, they'd also fashioned protective foot pads for their dogs. As for their horses, well, Ben guessed that an intelligent man would take the time to cut patches of leather or a heavy quilted saddle blanket and wrap his horse's fetlocks.

"Looks like I'm the one that's been the fool coming out here," he said out loud.

The night sky was studded with stars, but the moon was just a sliver of silver in the sky so that the light was not strong. That much, at least, was in his favor.

"We've got to reach the forest before they catch up with us," he said to his dogs. "If we don't, we're finished."

The dogs seemed ready. Ben took his bearings and decided that due west was the fastest way off the lava beds. If he could stay ahead of his pursuers and reach the forest before daylight, then he would have a chance of survival.

Ben took several minutes to cut up the rest of his shirt and wrap, then bind it around his moccasins. The soles of his feet were already bloody, but he knew that he could block out the pain and keep moving.

But it would be a race. "Old Scout," he said, "if things get bad, I might have to drop you and a couple of the others behind to fight those bloodhounds. But they're big dogs. Bigger than coyotes and as tough as wolves. Might be they'd kill you if the sheep-killing bastards that are driving them didn't do it first."

Old Scout listened to the baying cry of the bloodhounds, and he rumbled his challenge deep in his throat, then he turned and followed his master as they made a desperate try to reach the forest.

Chapter 16

"I think he is dead," Maria whispered the second morning that her husband did not return to their cabin. "If he were alive, he would be here."

Ki was dressed and on his feet. The poultices had drawn the poison out of his wounds, and he felt much stronger than he would have expected, given the condition he'd been in when he'd arrived with Ginger Brown.

Ginger looked at him. "You're still not in any condition to travel," she warned.

"Oh, yes, I am." Ki walked over to Ben Rodgers's wife and said quietly, "Your husband is being hunted by the same men who hunted Ginger and me. Tell me where he would have gone if they'd found him at Baldy Mesa."

"I don't know," she said. "Of course, he would have stayed far from this place."

"Exactly," Ki said. "And that's why I don't think we can assume he's dead. He may have had to go very far from here to lead the men from Alpine away."

Ki gathered his weapons and said, "I'm going to find and help him if there is still time."

"I want to go, too," Ginger said.

Ki went over to the young prostitute. "You need to stay with Mrs. Rodgers. It's possible men could show up here. If they did, you would be needed."

Ginger reluctantly nodded her head. "I'm just afraid for you, Ki. You've been through so much already."

"I will be fine," he said, touching her cheek. "You look fresh and clean, Ginger. This place must agree with you."

"I had forgotten how good I used to feel before I moved into town," she said. "Mind if I walk with you a little ways?"

"All right," he said.

"You must take a dog with you," Maria told him. "Even though they are still young, one of them in particular is very fond of my husband. If he is still alive, this Loco will help you find him."

"You are talking about the black one with the white circles around his eyes."

"Yes," she said. "My husband calls him Loco because the eyes look crazy. But he is the best of the bunch, and he will not slow you down."

"All right," Ki said. As soon as he had gotten directions from the woman that would take him to Baldy Mesa, he bid her good-bye and headed out the door, calling Loco after him. The dog was gangly but eager, and it seemed very happy that Ki had selected him alone to follow.

Ginger took the samurai's hand and walked him to the edge of the meadow. "I don't know that I shall ever see you again," she said. "I'm afraid for you."

"I will come back with Ben," he told her, thinking of how, away from Jake Hammer and Rosie's Place, she was blossoming just like a spring flower. Her hair had even started to shine.

"I want to give you something for getting me out of

Jake's mansion alive the other night," she said, picking a flower.

He started to reach for it, but she surprised him by unbuttoning her blouse, then slipping the stem of the flower between her breasts.

Ki chuckled. "Which is the present?"

"Take your pick," she said with a wink.

"I don't think I have time to do what I want to do."

"There is time," she told him with a wink. "It won't take long."

Ki took a deep breath and expelled it slowly as Ginger came to him and reached up, placing her fingers behind his neck. Very slowly she lowered his head to her breasts, which she gave a little shake, and pulled his face tight against her.

Ki decided that there was time. His mouth found her nipples, and she moaned with pleasure, then pulled him down to a bed of wildflowers.

Loco yipped and thumped his tail, but when he was ignored, he rested his head on his paws and watched as Ki opened Ginger as gently as he might the petals of a flower.

He now realized that he had wanted Ginger from the moment he had first seen her. He plunged his stiff rod into her, and even though she had known many men, she felt and looked like a wide-eyed virgin as she shuddered and kissed his face, then put her tongue in his ear and drove him half crazy.

"Yes," she panted, "I had nothing else to give you except this."

Ki's hips moved around and around as the woman's hard young body milked him expertly. He groaned with pleasure. "This is more than I expected. The flower would have been enough."

"Not for me," she said with a laugh.

150

For the next twenty minutes the samurai used all of his lovemaking skills to keep from exploding inside the woman beneath him. He stirred Ginger as if his rod were a giant spoon and her womanhood was a batter of warm butter. When she began to buck and lose control, he slacked his stirring until she shivered with delight and her kisses covered his face.

"Where did you learn to use a woman so well?" she asked breathlessly. "*I'm* supposed to be the expert at this."

"Maybe you've already lost your professional touch and become a new woman."

"That must be it," she panted. "Because what you're doing to me inside feels like when I first tried this in a hayloft at the age of fifteen."

Loco whined softly and padded over to lick Ginger's bare foot, which made her giggle. But then the young dog walked away, and Ki began to piston in and out of Ginger until her giggle turned to a moan and then a cry of pleasure as she lost control and her body joined his in a wild frenzy that ended with both of them grunting and bucking for release.

Ki's big rod jerked in and out, and he filled the woman as she clung to him on the bed of wildflowers.

He held her tight for several long minutes, then he climbed off of her and looked down at her white, lush body framed by the grass and the flowers. "What a beautiful picture," he said.

She smiled and looked up at him with his great wet manhood glistening stiffly in the sunlight. "Yes," she said, "it is. Come back soon, okay?"

"I will," he said, pulling on his pants and somehow managing to stuff his manhood back into his pants, where it bulged suggestively.

Ki took one last, lingering look at the beauty, and then

turned and left her lying naked in the meadow. It was hard to leave something like that, but it just gave him all the more reason to find Ben Rodgers and make a hasty return.

Later that same afternoon Ki smelled the presence of death five miles south of Baldy Mesa. Then he saw the vultures wheeling overhead, and he knew that he would find rimrocked sheep and perhaps the body of Ben Rodgers.

Ki was right on the first guess, and when he saw the two thousand bloated, broken bodies of sheep, he stood for a moment and shook his head at the pathetic waste of it all.

An hour later he had finished his grisly inspection, and even though his heart was saddened by the death of men, dogs, and sheep, he took some grim satisfaction in discovering that Ben was not among the dead and that the giant had exacted a very respectable toll on his enemies.

"Which way would he go?" Ki asked himself. "Which way would he go?"

He reasoned that Ben would have sought escape off the mesa by an avenue that would carry him even farther away from the log cabin where Maria and the pups were waiting. Ki found the steep trail that Ben had used to flee off the mesa, and then he took up the trail with Loco finally seeming to understand that this was a chase.

By nightfall he was into the lava beds and by the next morning, he had turned his back on that awful place and limped into the forest, removing his own little leather boots from Loco's sore paws.

Ki was swift and the pup had to run with great determination in order to stay up with him. Actually, it was not a pup, but neither was it a mature dog. Loco was probably six months old, but large and strong for its age.

As the samurai moved swiftly in pursuit of Ben and the men who hunted him on horse and with dogs, he wondered how he would attack. Unfortunately, he did not have his samurai bow and quiver full of arrows, but there were six of the shiny and deadly star blades hidden in his clothing. And he had the *surushin* and the *nunchaku* for close fighting.

The next night Ki heard the baying of the bloodhounds and Loco whined softly.

"They're close," the samurai said. "You must be very quiet or I will have to muzzle you. Is that understood?"

In reply Loco yipped with excitement and shot off into the darkness before Ki could grab him.

"Damn!" the samurai uncharacteristically swore. "That is not what I needed."

Ki took out after the pup, moving as fast as he could in the moonlight, and when he saw that it was heading straight for a huge canyon, he guessed that this was the place Ben had chosen to make at least a temporary stand against his pursuers.

He lost sight and sound of Loco until he neared the high-sided canyon, then he heard the sounds of a brief dogfight, followed by the yip-yip of Loco as the pup beat a hasty retreat back toward the canyon's mouth.

The pup was in full flight and about ten yards ahead of the two bloodhounds when he shot past Ki and out the canyon.

A moment later a man on a dark horse came racing after them, and Ki figured that this was as good a time as any to make his presence known. Unwrapping his *surushin* rope, he whirled it overhead and then let it fly just as the rider burst through the canyon mouth. His aim was true and the *surushin* wrapped itself around the rider's neck, causing him to drop his reins and fight wildly for breath.

The horse stepped on its reins and veered sharply to the

right, and Ki was there to grab it. The rider was strangling to death and his terror was so great that he didn't even notice the samurai until he was knocked from the saddle and rendered unconscious with a hard chop to the base of his neck.

Ki unwound the *surushin* and saved the man's life, though he had no doubt the favor would not have been reciprocated if he were the one being choked to death. He unbuckled the man's gun and strapped it around his waist. Ki greatly preferred his samurai weapons, but this was no time to be choosy. He also pulled the unconscious man's Stetson down on his own head and exchanged shirts, figuring they would give him enough of a disguise to ride back into the posse's camp without being recognized, given the additional aid of darkness.

The last thing Ki did before catching up to the riderless horse was to drag the limp body back behind the rocks. That finished, he straightened up just in time to see the bloodhounds reappear.

He reached for his knife, but the larger of the dogs wagged its tail ever so slightly and Ki relaxed. The dogs were working on scent, and he smelled like the cowboy who'd been chasing after them. "Come here, boys," he said in a gentle voice. "I won't hurt you."

The bloodhounds proved to be very friendly. They had been made to understand that they were on Ben's trail and that of his sheepdogs, so they had no animosity toward the samurai who caught them up and then used his *surushin* to tie them to a stout tree.

"Now," he said, looking back out of the canyon. "What did you do to Loco? Eat him? He was only a pup."

In reply, the bloodhounds flopped down in the dirt and showed him no further interest. They closed their eyes and gave every indication they were ready to take a snooze after their exciting chase.

With the dogs out of his way, Ki mounted the unconscious man's horse. There was a carbine in the boot, and between it and the sixgun, Ki figured he would be just fine if he were challenged in the darkness.

But his intention was to skirt the posse and move up the canyon in an attempt to reach Ben alone. If he could do that, and somehow avoid being killed by the old mountain man before he was recognized as a friend, then perhaps the pair of them, with a rifle, a sixgun, and six *shuriken* star blades could whittle down the odds pretty well before dawn.

Just as he was about to ride into the canyon, he heard a low growl from the darkness. "Loco?"

The half-grown sheepdog, every hair on its back, came walking on its toes in a wide circle around the two bloodhounds, who surprisingly did not seem at all interested in the intruder now that the issue of their supremacy had been firmly established.

The samurai stepped down from his horse. He grabbed Loco and threw him up behind the saddlehorn and then remounted. "Make one sound to give us away, and I'll throttle you," he said.

In answer, Loco licked his hand, and his tail thumped up and down on the samurai's leg as Ki rode boldly forward, praying that he would find the giant alive and able to fight.

Chapter 17

Ki rode very slowly, every nerve taut as he guided the horse back up the canyon toward the campfire of his enemies. When he could see them in the light, he lowered his head a little and kept coming.

"What you got there?" a man called.

Ki said nothing. Loco whined softly because he could feel the tension.

"You find out what stirred the bloodhounds up?" a man called.

The samurai shook his head and reined his horse toward a rope corral where the posse's horses were kept.

"Well, what the hell did you find out there!"

Ki kept riding.

"Say, what the . . ."

Ki saw the man reach for his gun. The samurai knew he had run out of time, and he slammed his heels hard against the horse's flanks. His mount shot forward into the rope corral, and suddenly there was pandemonium as horses stampeded in every direction.

A gunman who had been guarding the horses appeared

out of the darkness, and his gun flashed. Ki heard the whip-crack of the man's bullet past his ear, and he hurled a *shuriken* star blade.

The gunman pumped a bullet into the earth and then another straight up into the sky as the samurai, still clutching Loco, stampeded the posse's horses straight up the canyon.

It was a wild, hair-raising scramble over rocks and through brush and deadfall. Bullets were tracing the air after him, but through it all, Ki was most concerned that old Ben Rodgers would mistake him for an enemy and put a rifle ball through his heart.

He needn't have worried. With Loco yelping, the giant made no mistake, and when he jumped out in front of Ki's horse, he grabbed the reins and then yanked the Winchester out of the scabbard.

"Get up into those rocks yonder!" he shouted, levering a shell into the chamber and firing once just to let the men down the canyon know that he was fully armed again.

Ki tied his horse, then went racing after another loose animal. He grabbed it by the forelock, and the panicked creature slung its head and lifted him completely off the ground.

The samurai hung on until Ben rushed over and grabbed the frightened beast by the ear and twisted hard. Stunned with a sudden and excruciating pain, the horse froze while Ki ran to get a rope.

"You sure know how to arrive in the nick of time," Ben said, grinning broadly and holding the rifle up in the moonlight. "Them boys were about to finish me and my dogs off come daybreak. I was out of ammunition with my back to the wall. How much ammunition you bring along?"

"Whatever is left in the carbine and this sixgun I took from one of them."

Ben's smile slipped a little, but he said, "It'll do, friend. I figure that we might as well pay 'em a little visit once they settle back down around that campfire. They aren't fool enough to come searching for their remuda with us up here ready to shoot the shorts off 'em. What do you say?"

"Sounds like the smart thing to do," Ki said. "We're badly outgunned and outnumbered. I think our only hope is to attack in the darkness."

"Glad you agree. What we'll do is put the fear of God in their hearts—along with a few bullets. Tell you one thing, I sure didn't expect you to be up to coming to help out. You recover as fast as any man I ever saw."

"It was those scalding poultices you used on me," Ki said. "The idea of facing up to any more of those was just the thing I needed to get me up and moving."

Ben laughed. "And I see that Maria sent Loco along to sniff me out."

"Yes." Ki grew serious. "I'm sorry about your flock being rimrocked. I know how painful that must have been to watch."

The giant's face stiffened with bitterness. "I know that it's hard to understand for anyone but a sheepman, but those woollies were like my children. Sure, they were stupid and their damn bleatin' could get on your nerves, but I understood that when I went into the sheep business. And besides, the dogs are the ones that took it real hard."

"When this is over," Ki promised, "you'll have the money to buy more sheep. I know that Jessie isn't going to let Jake Hammer and his minions get away with all this."

The giant reached down and scratched Loco's ears. The young dog was obviously happy to see his master. "This one here," Ben said. "He's got the makin's of a leader. He's gonna take Old Scout's place at my side some day. You wait and see."

Ki had no intention of waiting, but there wasn't much sense in admitting the fact, so he just kept his mouth shut.

Ben stretched out on the ground and gazed up at the stars. "Man can never look too long up at heaven."

Ki smiled. "When I was a boy, things weren't too good for me. My mother and father had died, and I was an outcast in Japan. I used to pretend that the stars were pieces of candy, and I'd dream about eating them all some day."

"Bet that didn't go a long way toward filling your gut," Ben said. "Couldn't you hunt up some possum or rabbit? Maybe shoot a deer or something?"

"No," Ki said. "In Japan, only the royalty hunt, and the forests are off-limits to the commoner. I did get to be a pretty good fisherman. I fished in both streams and in the ocean."

"I never even seen an ocean," Ben said. "I expect they're mighty big and pretty. Salty as the Great Salt Lake, I hear. You know, a man can't drown in that lake. He can't even keep his body under water! Is it thata way in the ocean?"

"No," Ki said. "Each year many fishermen are drowned at sea. In Japan I remember they had typhoons."

"Ty-whats?"

"Typhoons," Ki said. "They're like cyclones or tornadoes only they come in over the water. They capsize boats and cause huge tidal waves that roll over the seaport towns and drown entire villages."

"Fools ought to know better than to live on low ground," the old man grunted. "Be as dumb as me sleeping in a dry riverbed during a driving rainstorm."

Ki studied the old man. Ben was not the most sympathetic or understanding man that Ki had ever known. To Ben, and men of his ilk, things were either right or wrong,

159

black or white, and subtle distinctions between the two were either ignored or discounted entirely.

"Things are a little different over there," Ki said quietly. "It'd be kind of hard to explain how everyone isn't exactly equal, like over here."

"Hell," Ben snorted. "Folks ain't equal here, either! Sheepmen ain't equal to cattlemen. Mexicans and Indians ain't treated equal to white men. Nor are women to men. You being half Chinaman, you oughta know that better than me."

Ki shook his head. "How soon shall we ride?"

"Why? You hungerin' for a fight?"

"Nope. I just would like to settle this issue and be done with it. I'm worried about Jessie, and I'd like to find her."

"What about that Ginger woman that brought you to our cabin? Bet you'd like to get back to that as soon as you can, huh!"

Ki smiled self-consciously. "I wouldn't mind," he admitted.

Ben stood up. "You take the saddle horse and I'll take the bareback one. We'll ride as slow and easy as we can until they see us, then we'll charge through the lot of 'em and when we reach the mouth of that canyon, we'll take firing positions and shoot up the whole damn bunch of them unless they surrender. Sound like a good plan?"

"It's uncomplicated, that's for sure," Ki replied. "Let's go."

They mounted their horses. Ki had the sixgun in his fist, and Ben had the Winchester carbine. He hadn't bothered to count the number of bullets in the magazine, and Ki guessed it didn't matter anyway. Their only chance at success was to hit their enemies and hit them hard and fast.

• • •

160

Just before they started down the canyon, Ben called his dogs around him and his horse. "It's every one of us boys —young and old—has got to look out for ourselves," he said quietly. "I don't know where them big bloodhound bastards are, but . . ."

"They're tied up at the mouth of the canyon," Ki said. "They won't be a problem."

"Good. Damned if I could stand to ride away from a dogfight if I thought my friends was gettin' eaten. Dogs, not a sound until I give a wild Comanche whoop. You understand?"

The dogs wagged their tails furiously, and it was clear that they were ready for some excitement. Ki was, too. Reining his horse in beside that of Ben, he glanced out of the corner of his eye and saw that the old man was smiling to himself. The Winchester looked like a toy in his huge hands. But it was anything but a toy.

Down the canyon they rode, and now Ki wished that the moon was not so large and illuminating. The campfire of their enemies was like a beacon, and it drew them like moths to a flame.

They were about a quarter mile from the fire when someone stepped out from the camp and came walking toward them.

One of the dogs growled low in his throat.

"Shhh!" Ben hissed.

The growling died.

Another hundred yards and they saw the man stop and pull down his pants, then squat.

Ben chuckled. "Just like a sittin' hen, ain't he?"

Ki didn't have an answer and there wasn't time for one anyway because Ben hissed, "Old Scout, sic him!"

The big male sheepdog hurled forward like a furry missile. Across the hard ground it flew silent and sinister, and when it leapt at the man, Ki heard a screech of pain and surprise.

Ben threw back his head and yelled, "YIP-YIP-HEEEE-TAI!"

It was his Comanche yell, and it did have a blood-chilling effect that sent the dogs into a frenzy, and that's when all hell broke loose.

Ki and Ben shot forward with their weapons blazing, and a few yards ahead of them the pack of sheepdogs flew at the men like demons. It was the sheepdogs that really struck terror into the camp. The dogs seemed demented with fury at the men who had rimrocked their charges. Ki saw men on their backs rolling around and trying to protect their throats.

Ki fired his sixgun more with the idea of scattering his enemies than killing them. But Ben did not share that view, and every time his rifle crashed, a man seemed to fall.

As Ki's horse swept through the camp, a man jumped at his reins, and the horse's shoulder struck and seemed to break him in half and throw him aside like some castoff rag doll.

But his horse stumbled, and the samurai was thrown to the ground. He hit and tucked in his right shoulder and rolled, coming up to his feet just as a man lunged at him with a knife.

Ki used a *yoko-geri-keage*, a "sideways sweep kick." He sent the power of his body through the kick, and when his foot shot out, it was in line with his waist and its hard edge was angled like the blade of a sickle as it smashed the man's kneecap and dropped him howling to the ground.

Another enemy fired at Ki, but missed, and before he could aim and pull the trigger again, Ki used the *shuto-uchi* or "knife hand" blow to knock his pistol spinning away in the darkness. Ki followed up with a powerful sweep lotus kick to the man's throat, and he went down choking.

Ki's hand flashed out from his shirt, and a star blade spun a deadly path into the body of yet another one of the enemy, and he could hear the roar of Ben's rifle, close and angry.

"Drop yer hardware!" Ben shouted. "Drop your guns, or we'll kill the lot of you!"

Ki whirled in time to see a man raise his gun, and the samurai delivered another star blade. The gunman's hand slapped his forehead, and he crashed over backward.

"Dogs!" Ben shouted. "Here, dogs!"

The sheepdogs appeared on command, and Ki quickly disarmed the men that were just wounded.

"How many?" Ben asked.

"Six is all."

"Line 'em up," Ben said.

Ki lined the men up without any difficulty, and the dogs rumbled in their throats.

"What are you going to do with us?" a man said.

"Kill you unless you're willin' to walk to Prescott and tell the politicians there who paid you to come hunting me down."

"Walk to Prescott! You must be—"

Ben rammed the barrel of the Winchester into the protesting man's belly.

"All right!" he gasped. "We'll talk! I ain't dying for Jake Hammer."

"Where is Buck Timberman?" Ki asked.

There was silence until Ben jammed his rifle into the same man's gut. "He went to find you and Ginger. He took one Apache and left us the other one."

Ki said, "There's no Indian here."

"Then he musta slipped out and run for it!"

Ben looked to Ki. "I got to go help Maria," he whispered.

"We're both going," Ki said. "We take their horses and boots. I don't think they'll be walking too far."

"You can't do that!"

Ki shrugged. "Then I guess I'll have to let old Ben shoot you. Either way, it makes no difference to me."

Without another word their captives began yanking off their boots.

"If Timberman and those Apache find Maria and harm a hair on her head, or of that other girl," Ben swore at the men, "I'll come back and shoot you men down like coyotes."

The men exchanged fearful glances. One of them said, "I never signed on to kill no woman."

"That doesn't matter to me," Ben said. "Which way did they go?"

"South," a rancher said. "Buck figured if you was leading us north, then your cabin had to be south somewhere."

Ben paled a little, and then he whipped the horse he was riding into a run.

Ki hesitated, then looked at the survivors. "I can't promise you I'll be able to stop him if Timberman has harmed or taken his wife. My suggestion is to move as fast as you can in all directions *but* south."

They nodded, and then, barefooted and unarmed, they scattered out from the mouth of the canyon like a flushed covey of quail.

★

Chapter 18

Buck Timberman stopped at the edge of the clearing and followed the pointing finger of his Apache scout. For a moment he did not see the cabin nestled deep in the shadowed woods, but then it seemed to take form.

The Apache tracker looked at Timberman and made a sign that he wanted to be paid and allowed to go.

"I got no money on me," the marshal said, shrugging his wide shoulders. "You go to Mr. Hammer. He'll pay you."

But the Apache either did not understand or did not want to understand. He shook his head violently and pointed at Timberman. "You pay!" he grunted.

"I said I got no money!"

"I take horse."

The Apache started for the horse, but Timberman grabbed his arm and shoved him away. "You touch my horse, my saddle, or any damn thing of mine, and I'll kill you," he growled.

Timberman stood almost a head taller than the Indian, but the Apache did not care. Drawing his knife, he lunged forward and the marshal's hand streaked to his gun. Only at the very last instant did he realize that he could not afford to fire a shot that would be heard in the cabin.

So instead of pulling the trigger, the marshal slashed the barrel of his pistol down hard. But the Apache was cat-quick, and he ducked sideways at the last instant so that the blow struck him on the shoulder instead of the head.

Timberman's other hand swatted at the knife, and then their bodies came together and they were rolling in the pine needles, each fighting for his life.

The marshal's superior strength and size allowed him to roll onto the Apache, and with the wrist of the Indian's knife hand locked tightly, he again slashed down with his pistol, and this time the barrel caught the Indian across the bridge of his nose, breaking it and dazing him. Blood must have poured down his throat because he began to choke.

Timberman brought the gun whistling down again, and it thudded dully against the Apache's forehead.

The marshal rolled off the Indian and stared down at his bloody face. "You should have done like I told you," he spat. "Hammer might have paid you."

But the Indian was dead, so Timberman turned his back on the man and wearily mounted his horse. He rode in a wide circle around the meadow and came up behind the house where he saw Maria chopping wood and Ginger Brown hauling it inside. The two women were talking animatedly, and the marshal grinned. It looked like the kind of scene he'd witnessed a thousand times in towns all over the West.

"Well, well," he said, drawing his gun and riding out of the trees. "It looks just homey as hell hereabouts."

Maria dropped the axe and started to dash for the cabin, but Timberman unleashed a bullet that took a big piece of bark off the cabin and left a white patch of wood.

"Next shot," he said, "will paint your brains on that little white spot. You better just turn around slow and easy. You, too, Ginger."

Ginger's eyes smoldered with hatred. "What are you doing here, Buck!"

"Oh, I thought I'd pay you a little visit. Besides, you're still the best-looking woman in this part of the country. Mr. Hammer, he misses you plenty. He wants you back, Ginger."

"I don't want to go back! I'm through with that."

"No, you're not," he said as patiently as if he were talking to a petulant child. "Once a whore, always a whore. You'll stay with Mr. Hammer until he tells you you're too old, and then he's promised he'll let me use you a year or two. When I hand you down to somebody else, you'll be finished."

Ginger visibly shivered and Maria came over to her side. "He is a snake," she hissed. "Believe nothing he says."

The marshal laughed outright. "You must be old Ben's woman. Figures he'd marry a Mexican. No white woman would have him."

Maria stiffened, and then she walked up to the marshal and spat in his face.

"Goddamn you!" he swore, backhanding her viciously into the cabin wall.

The pups, which had up to this moment been wagging their tails, now began to growl.

"Call them off!" the marshal yelled. "If one of them tries to bite me, I'll shoot the whole lot of 'em!"

Maria called the pups away, scolding them and making them go around the cabin.

"That's better," Buck said. "I expect some cooperation."

"What do you want!" Ginger cried. "If it's me, I'll come with you. Just leave this woman alone!"

Buck shook his head. "How very noble of you! Where is Ben and the samurai?"

"We don't know," Ginger said. "They left several days ago and haven't returned."

"Why did they leave?" His voice was lazy and conversational.

Ginger clamped her mouth shut, but when Buck raised his gun and pointed it at her, Maria said, "They went to fight you and save the flock."

"Flock is dead. We rimrocked your sheep. Every last one of them. Surprised you can't smell them from here when the wind is blowing just right."

Maria blinked. "My husband would never have allowed such a thing to happen."

"Your husband is just one old man," Timberman said harshly. "He can't cut the mustard anymore. Why, he's probably been run down by bloodhounds and is dead by now."

"I don't believe you!"

"Ain't important that you do," Timberman drawled.

"What are you going to do with us?" Ginger asked.

"I'd like to climb between both your legs, but I guess I better eat and get you back to Alpine first."

"Please," Ginger said. "Just leave this woman."

"Nope. I'm taking you both back to Alpine. Just in case."

"In case what?"

"In case Ben got lucky and escaped. If he did, then he'll come looking for his woman, and we'll be waiting for him," Timberman said, walking forward to grab them both and shove them toward the cabin door. "Let's go inside, and you can cook me a good meal before we leave."

An hour later Timberman's fierce appetite was satisfied, and he was ready to leave. He glanced at the fire that Maria had used to cook his lamb chops, and then he pushed back from his chair and said, "There any horses around here you can ride, or are you going to have to walk?"

"No horses," Maria said.

"Fine," Timberman said. "You both look like you're in good shape for a hike. So grab what you can carry and let's go."

Maria took little and Ginger had nothing but the clothes she wore. Timberman watched them closely, and when they were ready, he said, "Maria, just in case old Ben is alive, and he can read, maybe you better leave him a good-bye note. Tell him to come looking for you in Alpine."

She raised her chin. "My husband will know where to find me—and also you."

Timberman chuckled at that because he liked a woman with spirit, and the Mexican was a damn spirited as well as fine-looking mare. Not that he'd ever have admitted that to Rodgers. Hell, no! He hated the giant sheepman's guts, and because of it, when the women had gone outside, he went over to the stove and used a heavy ladle to push the fire out of its hearth and onto the wooden floor.

The coals spilled across the carefully cut and smoothed planks and then began to smoke. They'd be starting a full-blown fire within ten minutes, and within an hour the whole damn cabin would be nothing but a pile of embers.

"All right," he said, getting his horse and mounting.

"Let's go, ladies. And I use that term pretty damn loosely."

Maria and Ginger started across the meadow toward Alpine. When they reached the opposite side, Maria turned and then her hand flew to her mouth. "You burned it!" she cried.

"Might as well," Timberman said, pleased by the stricken look on her face. "Ain't nobody ever coming back to live here anymore. Not you, not Ben. Now let's adios! You got a long, hard walk, and I want to be back in Alpine before midnight."

It turned daybreak before they reached Alpine, and even though the marshal was prodding the exhausted women to move faster, they were shambling with weariness when they arrived.

Buck's first thought was to take them both to his jail, then lock them up and wait a few hours until he was certain that Jake Hammer was up before calling a meeting. But on second thought he decided that the best thing to do would be to take the two women straight on to Jake's mansion and have someone rouse the man.

Decisions would have to be made quickly.

"Well, well!" a guard said with a smile as they approached the mansion's gate. "If it isn't the prettiest whore in Arizona come back to pay us a visit."

Ginger's eyes flashed, and when the guard tried to pinch her butt, she slapped his face hard enough to make his head jerk back. He balled up his fist and would have struck her if Timberman hadn't intervened. "She's the boss's woman. You better remember that, Johnson."

He touched his face. "She's still a whore to me. Who's the other one?"

Timberman walked past the man, saying, "You're being paid to guard the gate, not ask questions. So do your job.

We may have company pretty soon, and it won't be a social call."

"You wake up Mr. Hammer, he ain't going to be too sociable, either, at this hour!"

Timberman said nothing, but when a big mastiff came around the corner of the house and began to growl, he froze. "Ladies, this is a new one I never seen before. So don't move!"

Timberman turned his head ever so slightly. "Johnson, call the dog!"

The guard chuckled. "What's the matter, marshal?"

Ginger saw that the mastiff was going to charge. She could see it in his eyes, and she was terrified. As a child, she'd been attacked and mauled by a dog, and ever since, the sight and sound of a big dog with the hair on its back standing up filled her with terror.

"Ohhh!" she cried, spinning around to run.

The dog went for her, and as it leaped, Buck Timberman drew his gun and shot it through the side of the head. Ginger fainted at the guard's feet.

"Jeezus!" he whispered. "If she hadn't tried to run, it wouldn't have went for her."

Buck Timberman was so incensed that he grabbed Johnson by the throat and slammed his head through the wrought iron bars of the fence, almost ripping off the guard's ears. Then, when Johnson was stuck and screaming, the marshal stepped back and kicked his ass until he couldn't stand up any longer.

"You stupid bastard!" he shouted. "I ought to kill you!"

Jake Hammer, dressed in his pajamas, came flying out the front door onto his porch with a sixgun clenched in his fist. His eyes missed nothing as he took in the entire scene.

"Buck, that's enough! Who shot my new guard dog!"

Timberman swung around. "I did. He was going for Ginger."

Hammer looked at the fallen woman. "Did he get her?"

"No. She fainted."

"Who is that?" he said, pointing to Maria.

Timberman told him, then added, "I don't know if Ben Rodgers is dead or not. But if he ain't, then this is our bait."

"What do you mean, you don't know if he's dead or not!" Hammer said angrily. "You went out to hunt the man, didn't you?"

"Yeah, but he'd already gotten off Baldy Mesa when I caught up with the posse. They were tracking him, but I figured if I found his woman, I had the key."

Hammer was not pleased. "Guard, you're fired!"

The man was trying desperately to pull his head out from between the bars, but his ears were bleeding and swollen, and he wasn't having any luck. "Please," he begged. "I can't get out."

"Buck, pull him out and get rid of him."

"No!" Johnson screamed. "Don't let him . . . ahhhhh!"

Buck Timberman had no patience or sympathy. He grabbed the guard by the back of his cartridge belt and jerked him completely off the ground, tearing his ears half off in the process of freeing him.

Johnson rolled around in the dirt, hands clutching his ears until Buck began to kick him again, and then the guard crabbed out through the gate and ran for town.

"Buck!"

The marshal turned.

"You take the gate until I decide what to do."

"Me? But I'm the town marshal!"

"Do it or I'll have your badge! And get that dead dog off my property."

172

Timberman swore as Hammer came down and picked Ginger up, then said, "Mrs. Rodgers, you follow me if you know what's good for you. There's still another dog on the premises. And he's meaner than the one Buck shot."

Maria followed them into the mansion and down a long corridor to a library, where he dumped Ginger onto a satin-covered love seat. He went over to a small, antique bar and poured a drink of brandy, which he attempted to pour down Ginger's throat.

When she sputtered and choked into wakefulness, he slapped her twice and very hard.

"Stop it!" Maria cried.

Hammer stepped back. "Nobody leaves Jake Hammer! Especially not a common, everyday whore!"

Ginger was awake now. "Oh, yeah?" she said, wiping her mouth. "Well, I left you, and the next time I leave you, I hope you're dead!"

Hammer glared at her. "Who is it? The samurai, or Mando? Or both? I'm sure you've had them every way imaginable."

Ginger swallowed. "What are you going to do now, Jake?"

He went over and poured himself a drink. He threw it down and said, "I'm going to call in some debts and get my friends to help me. We're going to have a party here, and while you women are entertaining men up in my bedroom, we'll just wait and see who comes to save your ass."

"No!" Maria swore. "I would rather die first!"

"That's your choice," Hammer said with a thin smile. "But you're still frisky-looking, and I'll bet you'd enjoy a good time in a real bed with silk sheets. Better think it over, señora. You'll be dead forever."

Chapter 19

When Jessie and Mando had finally reached the Santiago Ranch, they learned that Ben Rodgers's wife and Ginger Brown had been returned to the big Hammer mansion by Buck Timberman.

"What about Ki and Ben?" Jessie asked the Mexicans. "Has anything been seen of them?"

"They were being hunted to the north, up by the big mesa country," one of the Santiago men said. "Señor Rodgers's sheep were all rimrocked off Baldy Mesa."

Mando said, "We could go after Ginger and Señora Rodgers in Alpine."

Jessie shook her head and looked to Mando. "More likely we'd only succeed in getting ourselves killed. No, we've got to find out if Ki and Ben are alive."

Mando nodded. "We will need fresh horses. I know where the Rodgerses' cabin is to be found."

They left early the next morning, and by noon the following day they were almost to the cabin. "It is just over the hill and across a meadow," Mando said.

A few minutes later they were standing face to face with

Ben Rodgers and his rifle. The moment the giant recognized them, he lowered his weapon, and then Ki also materialized from cover.

Jessie was so relieved to see her samurai that she jumped from her horse and rushed over to hug his neck. "I was afraid that you were dead."

"And I was afraid that *you* were dead," the samurai told her. "I was torn between leaving Ben and going off to find you, or staying and trying to end this."

Jessie touched his face. "Thank heavens that you didn't leave. Now we can all fight together."

Jessie turned to study the legendary sheepman she'd heard so much about. He was as rough as the country that he claimed. "Mr. Rodgers, I'm sorry things have gone so badly for you up to now. I know about your sheep, and I can see what they did to your cabin."

Ben shook his head. "All I ever asked was just to be left in peace. That's all any of the sheepmen up here asked. We didn't want trouble. We just wanted to keep our ranches and have a chance to grow. But when the cattle prices started falling, the cattlemen got greedy and began to overstock their own ranges. Pretty soon they figured that they needed to take over ours."

"And since most of them were Spanish land grants," Jessie said, "it seemed easy enough to justify their greed."

Mando's eyes flashed. "They had nothing when they came except a need for the land. But they built their ranches, and we did not run them off when they were weak and we were strong. My forefathers *helped* the cattlemen many times. And now this is the way they try to repay our fathers' kindness."

"It's our payback time now, though," the giant sheepman growled. "When they killed my sheep, shot my dogs, and then took my woman, they crossed the line. I'm gonna break Buck Timberman's neck, and then I'm going to get even with Hammer."

Looking at the huge, enraged sheepman, Jessie didn't doubt that he could break a full-grown horse's neck. The only problem was that he made an awfully large target. He'd been successful in fighting cattlemen for a lot of years, but it had always been on his own terms. On *his* land and using *his* mountain man skills of tracking and survival. Jessie wanted to somehow bring this out to the man.

"We'll be going into Alpine, where Hammer runs things, and it won't be the same as shooting enemies from deep in the forest."

Ben studied her for a long moment. "I've slipped into Alpine on a few cold nights. Even made a friend or two there. Besides, killin' is killin'," he said. "And a man either hits what he shoots at on the quick, or he misses and dies. Those things don't change with the scenery."

"I just don't want you barging in there and getting killed," Jessie said. "You lost your sheep and your cabin, but you've still got a wife and those dogs to look after. And one more thing, when this is over, I'm going to see that you're compensated by Jake Hammer for all you've lost."

"The only compensation I want from that man is to see him dead," Ben told her solemnly. "And I can handle that by myself."

When the big man trudged away, Jessie looked at Ki and Mando. "He's going to get himself—and those women—killed," she said, "unless we watch him closely."

"I'll watch him," Ki said. "But I'll tell you something. He may be a large target and look slow, but he's not a man to take lightly. And if there is a long shot to be made by a marksman, he's the finest shot I've ever seen."

"That is true," Mando said. "But he was wrong when he

176

said that he would kill Jake Hammer. The man belongs to me!"

Jessie sighed. "Why don't we get to Alpine and size things up before we start arguing over who is going to kill whom?"

Mando said, "Hammer will have all the ranchers there to protect him."

"Well," Ben growled, "there's a whole bunch of his friends out walkin' barefoot in the forest that won't be there to help him. Ain't that right, samurai?"

"That's right," Ki said.

Jessie nodded. "Ki, you know the inside of the mansion. Where would Hammer most likely keep the women?"

"Upstairs," he said. "That's where the—"

He had started to say "bedrooms," but the expression on Ben Rodgers's face froze the word in his mouth. So instead, he amended, "the smaller locked rooms will be."

Everyone knew what Ki had been about to say and why he'd faltered and changed his wording. But they appreciated his intentions.

"Let's ride," Jessie said. "If we hurry, we can hit them at dawn."

The three men nodded. They were going to be badly outnumbered even despite the guns that Hammer had already lost. To Mando and Ben's way of thinking, that was the bad part. The good part was that after all these years of scraping and bowing to the likes of Jake Hammer, it was finally showdown time.

They rode stirrup to stirrup into Alpine from the north, and when they reached the center of town, they dismounted, tied their weary horses to a hitch rail, and made a final check on their weapons.

"I left my bow and arrows at the stageline office," Ki said. "I want them now."

177

"Bow and arrows?" Mando asked, his eyebrows raised in question. "But you got a sixgun."

"If he wants his bow and arrows, we'll wait," Ben said. "I seen him throw them little star blades, but I still can't believe my eyes. I expect I won't be able to believe what he can do with a bow and arrows, either."

Ki dashed over to the stage office, then used his knife to pry open the lock to the front door.

Jessie said, "Mando, Ki is better with guns than most westerners, but he prefers his own samurai weapons. He can unleash arrows quicker than most men can lever and fire their rifles."

"That I got to see."

They all saw the samurai get the door open, then disappear inside only to reappear a few minutes later with his bow and a quiver of arrows.

"Are they all right?" Jessie asked as Ki restrung the bow.

"They're fine," he said, testing the bow and then examining his arrows.

"Funny-looking thing, ain't it?" Ben said. "Kinda looks like it was built backward compared to the Indian bows I'm used to seeing."

"Wait until you see it in action," Jessie promised.

"Let's go," Ben said, starting for the mansion, whose lights they could see twinkling at the far end of town.

"Wait a minute!" Jessie said. "What we need to do is have some sort of plan."

"What the hell for!" Ben said menacingly.

"Because if we don't, there is every likelihood that Hammer will simply threaten to kill Ginger and Maria if we don't surrender."

Ben scowled and his big shoulders sagged. "Yeah," he

reluctantly agreed. "You got a point there, ma'am. Guess maybe we better think this out."

"I've been in his mansion once before, and I should go in alone now," Ki said. "I could find the women and then signal with a lantern from a window to let you know."

"We'll *both* go in there," Mando said.

"Thanks for the offer," Ki said, "but you're not a samurai, nor are you skilled in *ninjutsu*, the art of the invisible assassin."

"No, I'm plenty visible," Mando said, "except when I'm hunting in the wood for deer or elk or hired gunmen. I can stay up with you, and I won't make a sound. Besides, with two of us, we have twice the chance of reaching the women."

"He's right," Jessie said.

"Okay," the samurai said. "But you follow me. Is that understood?"

"And if it isn't?"

Jessie stepped between them. It was clear that, because they were about the same age and size and both were proud of their physical abilities, there was some rivalry, especially in Mando's case.

"Both of you go in," Jessie said. "But Ki, you are in charge because you've already been in that mansion and know what to look for. Give us a signal when you have Ginger and Maria safely in hand."

Mando didn't like being placed under anybody, but he nodded. "Let's go."

Ki moved into the shadows, and Mando went right with him while Jessie and Ben began to advance through the dark, silent town.

Jessie said, "The nearest cover to the house is that livery barn up ahead. That's where we'll take up firing positions."

Ben nodded. "Sure wish I had my big Winchester instead of this carbine," he said. "But I'm still out of bullets."

"That thirty-thirty will do you just fine," Jessie said. "I wonder how many men Jake Hammer has gathered in that big house."

"Could be fifty, but more likely it's less than half that many."

"Let's hope it's a whole lot less than half that," Jessie said. "Look! They're going over that iron fence."

Jessie and Ben watched the two silhouettes as they scaled the fence and then vanished into the yard.

Ben shook his head. "Damn good thing that your samurai took Mando instead of me. Most likely, I'd have got my breeches hung up on the top of that fence and that's about as far as I'd get."

Jessie nodded absently. "I just hope they can reach the women before the alarm is sounded."

Ki hoped so, too, as he and Mando ran low to the ground and flattened themselves under a window. Ki raised his hands slowly to the window and pushed. It wasn't locked. "We've got to get inside," he said quickly. "There are big dogs patrolling this place."

"Then let's go."

Ki did not need urging. He pushed the window open and was inside in an instant, and Mando followed right behind. So far, so good.

"The kitchen," Mando said. "But they have some good food here, and I'm damn hungry."

"Later."

Ki moved to the door leading into the main part of the house. He slowly pushed it open and saw a pair of guards standing at the foot of a long staircase. They were sitting in chairs facing the front door.

Ki moved forward slowly with Mando right behind.

180

When he was almost on top of them, one of the guards started to turn to say something to the other, and the edge of the samurai's hand whistled downward to thud against the man's neck. The guard slumped over, and before Ki could grab it, the chair overturned loudly in the hallway.

Mando jumped at the second guard, and his pistol lashed down on the man's skull, dropping him.

"What's the ruckus in there!" someone shouted from a parlor off the hallway. "Hey!"

Ki whispered, "You go upstairs and try to find them now! I'll try and slow things down here."

"But—"

"Do as I say!" Ki hissed, shoving the Mexican toward the stairs as two more men burst into the hallway with drawn guns.

Ki had no time to bring his bow into play, so he went for a star blade and managed to kill one of the men before the second one got off a round. Fired inside the hallway, the sixgun sounded like a buffalo rifle. Ki heard Mando's boots pounding up the stairs, and then he heard a woman scream.

The samurai threw himself into a dark room, yanked an arrow from his quiver, and fitted it on his bowstring before jumping back out in the hallway and firing his weapon.

He had chosen "death's song" as his first arrow because it had a small, ceramic bulb with a hole through it which caught the air and made a shrieking sound in flight. Because the distance was so short, the shriek in this case was brief, and it ended with a cry of pain as a gunman clutched his chest and fell backward.

Ki sprung up the stairs and almost crashed into Mando, who had the two women at his side. "They heard the commotion and figured it was help coming!"

A deafening volley of gunfire was erupting up the stairwell, and it drove them back into one of the rooms.

"Light a lantern and make the signal to Jessie and Ben!" Ki shouted.

The signal was made, and a moment later gunfire from the town split the night. Mando raced to the door and emptied his sixgun to keep their enemies back while Ki searched for a way off the second floor.

"There must be twenty of them on the stairs!" Mando shouted, frantically reloading as they all heard men coming up the stairs.

Mando just did manage to reload and drive the gunmen back before his gun was empty again.

"Here!" Ki said, tossing his own sixgun to the sheepman. "Use this one while Ginger reloads the other."

Ginger was quick to understand her role. She reloaded as Mando fired, and Ki searched desperately for an escape from the room. He knew that there were too many gunmen to shoot their way down the staircase, and he was unwilling to see the women get riddled in such a desperate attempt to break out of the mansion.

But suddenly he saw Jessie and Ben charging across the street, firing their guns. Ki pulled his window as high as it could go, and when a guard raced around to reinforce the gate, Ki shot him from above. Then Jessie and Ben were breaking through the gate and into the house, guns blazing.

From the dark, hellish confusion of the stairwell, Jake Hammer was exhorting his men to fight. Bursting through the front door, Jessie saw him, and the man saw her and Ben at the same instant. Jessie fired from the hip and Hammer shivered in the gloom, but still raised his pistol. Ben's rifle drowned out everything, and Hammer's slug drilled him through the eye and exploded out the back of his head, his brains splattering the men and filling them with terror.

"Don't shoot!" one of them cried.

The others were of the same mind.

"Everyone throw down your weapons!" Jessie shouted. "And hit the floor!"

It was hard for grown men to "hit the floor" when they were all bunched up on the stairs, but somehow, they did. A moment later, Jessie saw Mando, Ki and the two women appear at the top of the stairs.

"Is everyone all right?"

"Yeah," Mando said. "It's over."

The next morning Jessie and Ki paid a visit to Judge Larson. They caught him hastily packing his belongings in a big trunk, and there was a buckboard ready and waiting out in back of his house.

"Going someplace?" Jessie asked quietly.

The judge's eyes widened in shock, but he quickly recovered enough to stammer, "That's none of your concern, Miss Starbuck!"

The gun in Jessie's fist cocked, and she said, "You've a bunch of men to sentence to the Yuma Prison this morning. And you're going to do a few other 'good deeds' to atone for the bad ones you've committed for so many years."

Larson licked his porcine lips. "What are you talking about?"

"I'm saying that you're going to pardon Mando Santiago, then rule in the favor of all the Mexican Spanish land grant holders. Finally, you're going to allow Ben Rodgers and all the other families damages that are to be paid from the sale of the cattle ranch and mansion previously owned by the late Jake Hammer."

"But those assets are not even on the market!"

"Not any more they're not," Jessie said. "Because I'm buying them, and the sale money will go to Ben and the other families that Hammer and his father before him persecuted all these many years. And your last official act before you resign your seat on the bench is to make all the paperwork legal."

Larson bristled. "You've got it all figured out, haven't you, Miss Starbuck."

"Not all of it," she said quietly. "I'm still trying to figure out how to sentence you to prison along with the others."

The judge paled. "I'll get the papers in order," he stammered. "I'll hold court today and I'll be out of town before the end of the week."

"You've got until sundown," Mando said. "And after that, it's varmit hunting season in this part of Arizona Territory."

The judge's hands began to tremble, then he started moving fast.

Watch for

LONE STAR AND THE RENEGADE RANGER

ninety-second novel in the exciting
LONE STAR
series from Jove

coming in April!